The Swede

The Swede

By
R.W. Nichelson
"Based on a True Story"

BookVenture Publishing LLC
1000 Country Lane Ste 300
Ishpeming MI 49849
www.bookventure.com
Hotline: 1(877) 276-9751
Fax: 1(877) 864-1686

Ordering Information:
Quantity sales. Special discounts are available on quantity purchases by corporations, associations, and others. For details, contact the publisher at the address above.

Printed in the United States of America

Library of Congress Control Number: 2017931088
ISBN-13: Hardback   978-1-946492-42-5
                 Paperback   978-1-946492-90-6
                 Pdf   978-1-946492-43-2
                 ePub   978-1-946492-44-9
                 Kindle   978-1-946492-45-6

Rev. date: 01/23/2018

To Dr. Lisa Vila for the motivation to finish the job and to my loving wife, Cheryl, for without her help and support this endeavor would not have been possible.

INTRODUCTION

DURING WORLD WAR II there were approximately some three hundred Swedish volunteers that joined the Waffen-SS, the actual count is unknown. These men did not necessarily join the German military to spread Nazi ideology, but to keep communism from enslaving the free countries of Europe one by one. This was the case for many of the foreign volunteers of the Waffen-SS. For most, this was the only option they had to play a part in the effort to contain the spread of communism and this is the remarkable story of two of those men. Though parts of this story were added for effect to some of the characters, the main theme of the story is based on actual events.

CHAPTER ONE

IN 1939 RUSSIA INVADED Finland in a conquest for land but the Finnish people were up for the fight. Finland had previously been under control of the Russians but they had won their independence from them years before. The occupation of Finland gave them a clear understanding of exactly what the Russians were capable of and they were not about to let this happen again. If the Russians were to win the war with the Finns, the people of Finland would be enslaved once again by a godless and cruel people. They were very determined to not let that happen again and put everything they had into the fight.

At the Russian front, just outside of Suomussalmi, Finland, two Russian soldiers kick in the door of a little country house. Inside the house a twelve-year-old girl was standing in the corner of the room playing with her dolls. Startled and afraid, the young girl attempted to run toward the front door in an effort to get away from the soldiers but one of them quickly stepped in front of her and slapped her across the face knocking the girl to the floor.

The girl's lip began bleeding from the blow to her face and she began to cry from both pain and fear. The soldier picked the young girl up from the floor and throws her on the table. The little girl kicks and screams as she is crying, trying to get away from the Russian soldier. The soldier easily overpowers the young girl and turns her over facedown on the table with her legs hanging over the edge. The soldier pulls up her dress, then pulls his pants down and grabs the little girl by her ponytail pulling her head back.

A shot rings out in the room and the Russian soldier falls to the floor, his head pumping out blood to the rhythm of the last beats of his heart. Hans Gruber stands at the door with his rifle in hand. Hans is a Swedish volunteer with the Finnish army and has a burning hatred for the communists. The second Russian soldier in the room reaches for his rifle and takes aim at Hans. He shoots at Hans and the round hits Hans in the side of his chest. Hans fires at the Russian soldier as he falls to the floor and bullet from his rifle hits the Russian dead center in his chest, killing him instantly.

Hans staggers over to the little girl, weak from his wound, and comforts her. Hans says to the girl, "Go to your mother and hide with her." The girl runs out the door and Hans faints from his wound and falls to the floor. Hans wakes up in a Finnish hospital confused not knowing where he is. Hans asks a nurse walking past his bed, "Miss, where am I?"

"You are in a hospital in Oulu, Finland," she answered.

"How long have I been here?" Hans asked.

"Three days and don't worry, you are going to be fine." The nurse said. Relieved at knowing where he was Hans relaxed and put his head back down on the pillow and quickly falls back to sleep.

Two weeks later an officer in the Finnish army presented medals to the wounded soldiers in the hospital for their heroism in combat. Hans received two awards for valor in hand to hand combat on the Russian front. Hans didn't know it but these two little medals would later save his life. Due to his wounds Hans was released from duty with the Finnish army. Hans went back home to Sweden and was celebrated as a hero. Though Hans thought the praise was great, he was just happy to be home and away from the war.

Hans had seen a lot of cruelty in the days he had been fighting the Russians. He had come to know them as a cruel and ruthless people that would kill and rape innocent women and children just for the thrill of doing so. The brutality he had witnessed ignited a burning hatred of the Russian communists and it gave him a great desire to fight them again, if he ever got the chance. Little did Hans know that he soon would.

In Germany, Hitler became chancellor in 1933 and had steadily been building his military into one of the largest in the world. In the late 1930s Hitler marched to Rhineland and acquired the Sudetenland on the border of Czechoslovakia then annexed Austria into the Fuhrer's Third Reich. In 1939 Hitler made a pact with Russia not to go to war with Germany if they invaded Poland. On September 1, 1939, Hitler, and then sixteen days later, Stalin, invaded Poland and divided the spoils between Germany and Russia.

A declaration of war from France and England for Germany's invasion of Poland soon followed suit. On May 10, 1940, Hitler invaded France using his blitzkrieg tactics. The German Army pushed the French army and the English expeditionary force in to the sea at Dunkirk, conquering France in just weeks. All Hitler had left to do was defeat the English and the war would be over, but Hitler had bigger fish to fry. The conquest of Russia was more important and England would have to wait. Hitler said, "We have only to kick in the front door and the whole rotten Russian edifice will come tumbling down." He would find it to be a greater challenge than he expected.

On June 22, 1941, Hitler with four point five million troops initiated Operation Barbarossa—the invasion of Russia. Hans read about the invasion in the paper, he became excited with the prospect of finally destroying the communist regime once and for all. Hans wondered to himself what he could do to be a part of this great and noble crusade. He walked into the kitchen where his mother was sitting and asked her, "Mom, did you hear about Germany invading Russia?"

"Yes I did, that's all they are talking about down at the market," Hans's mother replied.

"I am thinking about joining the German Army to go fight the Russians," Hans said.

"Why would you go and do that, the Germans are just as bad as the Russians, fascists and communists, what's the difference?" Hans's mother replied.

"The Germans are trying to create a better world, the Russians just want to enslave it. Besides, there is no work here and the Germans pay their soldiers well, at least more than I can make here." Hans said.

"You are a grown man now," Hans's mother said. "You can do as you wish. Just be careful son, I love you."

Hans wanted to enlist in the German Army but he wasn't sure he wanted to do it alone. He went to his friend Sven Eriksson's house to see if he would be interested in joining him on this great adventure. Sven had fought with Hans against the Russians during the Winter War of 1939 and like Hans, would love to get the chance to fight the communists as well. Sven had a great distain for the Bolsheviks and wanted to kill as many of them as he could, that is if he ever got the chance.

Hans got to Sven's house and knocked on the door, there was no answer. Hans knocked again this time harder and yelled, "Sven! Get your ass up!"

Sven slowly made it to the door and opened it. "What the hell do you want at this hour of the morning?" Sven asked. Hans could tell that Sven had been drinking all night, he does it quite often. Hans told Sven that he needed to talk to him so they went into the kitchen and sat at the table. Sven, holding a bottle of vodka asked Hans, "Would you like a shot?"

Hans said, "No, we don't have time for that nonsense now we need to have a serious talk. The Germans have invaded Russia."

"Really, I thought the Germans and the Russians had a pact not to go to war with each other?" Sven said.

"It's true," Hans said. "Do you want to go fight? We can enlist in the German Army. All we have to do is to travel to Norway and enlist there."

"That sounds like a good idea," said Sven. "My family could use the money." "Let's leave this following Monday," Hans said. "That will give us time to say goodbye to everyone."

There is someone in particular Hans wanted to make sure and say goodbye to, his girlfriend Carina. Carina and Hans had been a couple since elementary school and had planned to be married next spring. This would now have to be put on hold if Hans is going to war and Hans hoped that Carina would understand that he had to do this and that she would have to wait for his return before they could marry.

Hans walked down the dirt road to Carina's house, kicking stones along the way talking to himself, trying to figure out what he would say to her. "I have to plan out how I am going to tell her," Hans said to himself. "I will have it all together when I talk to her and hopefully she will understand." Hans reached Carina's house and knocked on the door. Carina answered. "Well, what a pleasant surprise. Come in and sit with me and have some tea."

"Carina, I must talk to you about something that is very important to me," Hans said.

"What is it?" Carina asked.

"The Germans have invaded Russia and I think I want to join the German Army to be part of this. It will be a chance to finally rid this world from communism," Hans said. "The Germans will pay me well and you know I haven't been able to find work here in over a year now and we desperately need the money." All the while he is explaining Hans is thinking that he couldn't wait to kill some of those communists but he would dare not say that to his Carina. Hans didn't want her to think he was cruel in any way.

"When would you leave?" Carina asked.

"We will go first thing Monday morning. Would you wait for me?" Hans asked her. "It will only be a few months and I am sure the war will be over soon and I will have a little money to get a place for us."

"Yes, I would wait for you but don't make me wait too long, buster," Carina said. "Don't be afraid, Sven is going with me," Hans said. We can keep each other out of trouble."

"I am more worried about Sven getting you in trouble. It's getting late, why don't you spend the night," Carina said. Normally it would not be acceptable for a young man to spend the night with an unmarried young woman but Hans has occasionally been staying the night there since they were both playmates in elementary school. Carina's parents didn't mind, he was already like a son to them. It was just a matter of formality to make it official.

The following morning Hans rose early to get started on the day. He kissed Carina on the cheek as she lay sleeping leaving her a note on the pillow. Hans got dressed and slowly creeped out of the door and walked down the road towards home. Hans needed to grab a few things for the trip and say goodbye to his mother. When Hans got to the house and opened the door, his mother was sitting in her rocking chair knitting a sweater for Hans. "Mother, I need to tell you something," Hans said.

His mother said that she already knew that he was there to say goodbye.

"How did you know?" Hans asked.

"A mother knows these things, my love."

"I love you, Mamma, and I promise to come home soon," Hans said. He went to his room and grabbed a few things to take with him then went to the kitchen and took two apples a half loaf of bread and some butter for the trip. Hans went to his mother and kissed her on the cheek. "I love you, Mamma, and I will be careful." Hans took his mother by the hand and walked to the door with her and his mother said, "I love you too, sweetheart. Please be careful."

"I will, Mamma, I promise." Hans walked out the door, as he did he yelled back, "I will be okay, Mamma, don't worry. I will send money." Hans blew his mother a kiss and was on his way.

As Hans walked away his mother fell to her knees sobbing knowing that this may be the last time she ever sees her boy again. She had gone through this nightmare before when he had joined the Finnish army in the Winter War of 1939. She prayed, "God, please take care of my son." Her hands grasped together in front of her as if she were begging her master and sat there crying as she watched her baby boy walk off to war.

CHAPTER TWO

Hans hurriedly walked to Sven's house. He was so excited thinking about this new adventure they were about to be on and he wanted to get it started as soon as possible. Hans got to Sven's house and helped him gather a few things that he might need for the trip, then the two boys headed to the railway station in Stockholm. Hans and Sven caught a ride on a vegetable truck to Stockholm. It had been a long time since they both had visited Stockholm so they decided to see the sites of the city while they had the opportunity.

The boys visited Gamla Stan (old center), Stadshuset (city hall), Sergels Torg (the plaza), and the Drottningholm (royal palace) and that evening got a hotel room for the night. Hans and Sven woke early the following morning and made their way to the railway station. The boys went directly to the ticketing booth and asked the man behind the counter "How much is a one way ticket to Oslo?"

"That will be four hundred kronor," answered the ticketing agent.

"I will take two, please," Hans said.

"The train will be leaving in ten minutes, you will just have time to make it," said the ticketing agent.

Sven asked Hans if he remembered the train ride in Finland during the war in 1939. "Yes," Hans said. Hans clearly remembered the cold winter air rushing in the boxcar as the train screamed down the track toward the battle lines. It was freezing cold and Hans thought to himself that he was grateful he would never have to go through that again. They boarded the train and settled down in their seats and got as comfortable as they could for the long ride. The boys would be in Oslo by morning.

The train came to a sudden stop at the border of Norway and Sweden. German guards were checking the papers of all the travelers on the train. Hans woke Sven and told him to get his papers that were needed to cross the border. The German soldiers were coming down the aisle looking at each passengers papers one by one coming closer and closer to Hans and Sven. Sven was scurrying around going through his clothes and what little he had brought with him to find his papers.

The German soldier walked up to where Hans and Sven were sitting and demanded their papers. Sven looked scared to death. The soldier ordered louder, "Papers, papers!" Sven finally found his papers in his coat and handed them to the soldier then sat back in his seat in relief. The soldier looked the papers over and quickly gave them back to Sven. "Be sure and have your papers ready at any moment, there are too many people to check and if you don't have them ready you put us behind schedule," the soldier said with a snarl. The solders then left the train and the train slowly started moving down the tracks again.

Hans said to Sven, "We are almost there, next stop Oslo." The train rolled in to Oslo and slowed down with an ear piercing screech of the railway tracks. This woke Hans and Sven from their sleep. The boys quickly gathered their things and got off the train. They had decided to go straight to the German Army recruiting center, but they weren't sure where it was. Hans asked the ticketing agent at the railway station where the recruiting center was. The agent said, "I don't know and I don't care." Then slammed his window shut.

"That was uncalled for," Sven said.

Hans agreed and said, "His wife must have pissed him off or something, what a grouch."

The two men headed down the street to Oslo, they came across a police officer and asked him where the recruiting office was. The officer said, "It is two blocks south and a block west of here, you can't miss it, it has two big SS flags in front of the building."

Hans and Sven quickly walked to the SS recruitment building. When they reached the recruiting office they saw two very large flags, one on either side of the entry way. They were black with two white lightning bolt SS on them.

Hans and Sven looked at each other and Hans said, "This must be the place." And they both went inside. They met a guard just inside the door and asked him where they needed to go to volunteer. The guard told them, "Go down the hall to the room on the left and see Obersturmführer (Senior Lieutenant) Shope, he sees all new inductees." Hans thanked the guard then he and Sven walked down the hall to the lieutenant's office and knocked on the door.

"Enter!" the lieutenant bellowed. Hans opened the door and walked in. "Lieutenant, I am Hans Gruber and this is Sven Eriksson, we would like to join the Waffen-SS."

"Well, well," said the lieutenant. "Where are you boys from?"

"We are from Sweden, sir," Hans told the lieutenant.

The lieutenant said, "We have had a few volunteers from Sweden and so far from what I have seen and heard they make very good soldiers. We can get you in a unit but first you must prove you are of Aryan decent."

"That will not be a problem," Hans said. "We know the history of both our families going back over one hundred years."

"Great," said the lieutenant. "Once we can verify that I see no problem in getting the both of you in, that is if you can pass the training requirements. Come back and see me tomorrow and we will start your processing."

"Yes, sir," Hans and Sven replied then turned and left the lieutenant's office.

"It looks like we will have to find a place to stay for the night," Hans said.

"Look! There is an inn just down the street and we could stay there," Sven replied.

"How convenient is that?" Hans said. "Things are looking up for us." They went to the inn and booked a room for the night. Hans noticed an attractive young woman sitting in the parlor and walked over to her thinking he might strike up a friendly conversation.

"Hi, what's your name?" Hans asked.

"My name is Aesa," the young woman replied. Hans stated that he would only be in town a couple of days and would sure appreciate it if she could show him around the city. She agreed and said, "I will meet you back here at seven in the morning to show you the local sites. Make sure you are here, I am a very punctual person." Aesa then abruptly walked out the door.

"Wow!" Hans said. "It looks like my luck keeps getting better and better."

Hans was eager to meet Aesa so the next morning he made sure that he was down in the parlor at six thirty, just in case. Hans couldn't wait to see her. Something about her was mysterious and magical and she seemed to have cast some sort of spell on Hans with just a few words from her mouth. Aesa showed up at seven, right on time. They had coffee and talked for a little while then headed out to see the town.

Hans and Aesa went to see the Norwegian Parliament, the National Theater, the Norwegian Royal Palace (Slottet) and the Olso Cathedral (Domkirke). The buildings were beautiful and Hans began to think about all the historical things they got to see and how lucky he was to get to see them with such beautiful company. It was getting late so Hans walked Aesa home. She lived in a simple flat above a café. "Can you stay?" Aesa asked.

"I am sorry, Aesa, I can't. I have a girl back home," Hans replied.

"Your girl is back in Sweden so it doesn't matter, you are in Oslo now. What she doesn't know can't hurt her," Aesa said seductively.

Hans just smiled and kissed her cheek. "I would love to. I truly would but I can't. Not sure if I could live with myself if I did." Hans thought about Carina, waiting at home for him and though the opportunity was there, he could not take advantage of it due to his love for her. Carina meant the world to him and he knew he could never betray her. Hans headed back to the hotel to get a good night's sleep, he knew the following day would be a long one for him so he went back to the hotel to make sure that he got plenty of rest.

The next morning Hans and Sven headed down to the Waffen SS recruiting center. There were two SS guards standing outside the building, they stared straight ahead not even looking at them as they walked in. Just inside the building was a desk where a husky oberscharfuhrer (sergeant) sat to receive recruits. The sergeant asked for their papers and looked them over. The sergeant asked, "Why do you want to join the Waffen-SS?"

"There has been a long hatred between the Swedes and the Russians and we want to get in the fight to get rid of those bastards once and for all," Hans said.

The sergeant looked the boys over and said, "Very good. I think you boys will do just fine. Go with Stabsgefreiter (Corporal) Shultz and he will take you to your physical and to get uniforms," Shultz said. Hans and Sven looked at each other and smiled. Hans said with a grin on his face, "We're in, buddy."

The sergeant behind the desk said, "Not so fast, recruit, you still have to pass the physical."

"No problem, we are in tip top shape," Hans said. Corporal Shultz then guided them to the back of the building for physical and processing.

As they were lead back Hans asked, "Sven, have you ever been through something like this?"

"Never, even when we joined up with the Finnish army, they just suited us up and gave us rifle s and pointed us to the front," Sven said.

"I am glad they are willing to do all these, at least this way we will know all our comrades will be in good health," Hans said.

"Come on boys, less talking and more walking, we have schedules to keep," Shultz said.

CHAPTER THREE

AFTER INDOCTRINATION HANS AND Sven were sent to Germany for SS training. Combat training consisted primarily of several months of intensive basic training with three objectives—political indoctrination, physical fitness, and small arms proficiency. One in three potential SS recruits failed to pass the course. During training Hans, Sven, and the rest of his training platoon was in their barracks filling magazines with cartridges. It was very quiet in the barracks, there was no talking allowed. All you could hear was the clicking sounds that were made from the men putting the cartridges into the magazines.

One of the young recruits across the aisle way from Hans dropped a cartridge on the floor. It makes its own distinct sound when it hits the floor, very different from the noise from loading the magazines. The sound caught the ear of the sergeant in charge of training and he immediately stood up from the chair he had been sitting while reading the paper. "Who the hell dropped a cartridge?" the sergeant bellowed.

"It was me, Sergeant," the young recruit said.

The sergeant quickly ran over to the recruit and stood in front of him. The sergeant's face mere inches from the recruit's face and began screaming at the young man. "Pick that cartridge up you worthless piece of shit. What the hell do you think this is, the Wehrmacht (the German Army)?" Insulting both him and the German Army.

"No, Sergeant!" the recruit yelled to the sergeant. The recruit quickly bent down to pick up the cartridge. The young man grabbed the cartridge and quickly stood up in front of the sergeant at attention.

"Not like that you idiot, get down and give me twenty pushups," the sergeant said pointing at the floor.

"Yes, Sergeant," the recruit said fearfully. The recruit then dropped to the floor. While the recruit was doing pushups he would count each one "one sergeant…two sergeant…"

The sergeant was screaming at him "You are a worthless piece of crap! Why the hell do you think you can be an SS soldier? I don't even understand why they would let a worthless piece of shit like you apply for the SS anyway." The recruit finished doing his pushups and stood up quickly in front of the sergeant.

"Get down and pick that cartridge up with your mouth," the sergeant said. The recruit dropped to the floor and quickly scooped up the cartridge in his mouth and stood up again before the sergeant. You could tell that the recruit was letting the sergeant get to him, his face was red and he was tearing up, on the verge of crying. Not the kind of mental toughness you need to have to be a combat soldier, it gets much worse than that on the front lines. "What the hell is this? The sergeant bellowed. "Crying? Why you big disgusting baby, you're no SS man. Get the hell out of my barracks!" The recruit quickly ran out the door, tears welling up in his eyes with the sergeant pursuing right behind him. Hans never saw that recruit again.

After basic training, Hans and Sven were sent to specialist schools where they received further training in their chosen combat arm. Hans and Sven were taken with the rest of their training platoon to get fitted for new uniforms. They both had loved the look of the SS uniforms and could not wait to get their own. After the fitting they were lead to the armory to receive their weapons. Hans stood at the armory door and a rifle flew at him from what seemed to be out of nowhere. He caught the rifle and a voice inside the armory said, "It feels good to have a rifle in your hands, doesn't it? Treat it like a lover, the bitch may save your life."

"Move your ass out, recruit!" the man behind the counter said pointing at the direction of the door. Sven was next and the armor threw the rifle at him as well. Sven caught the rifle but the sight at the end of the barrel hit him in the forehead and he started to bleed. "Son of a bitch," Sven said as he held his forehead in pain. The voice inside the armory shouted out the serial number of the weapon and said, "Suck it up, sweetheart. There is going to be a lot more blood than that where you're going." The sergeant then showed the platoon of men to their quarters for the night. There were rows of bunk beds in a very long room and they took the first two bunks closest to the door. The boys were exhausted and gratefully settled in for the night.

Hans and Sven were given a one week leave after training before they were to report to their combat units on the Russian front so they decided to venture to Berlin. They could hardly wait for the chance to see Berlin. It was a beautiful city and Hans figured they would probably never get to see it again so he would take it all in now while he had the opportunity. Hans and Sven caught a bus to Berlin with a sense of excitement in anticipation of the trip.

They both walked to the rear of the bus and had a seat in the last row. "I'm going to see all the sites while in Berlin," said Hans. "Do you want to go with me or do you have other plans?" Hans asked. Sven looked and Hans with a "cat got the canary" smile said, "No, I have other plans, I am going to find me a girl and get drunk for a week."

"Well, that definitely sounds like you, Sven," Hans replied and raised his eyebrows in a look of sarcasm.

"Not me," Hans said. "I have to save every *reichsmark* (dollar) I can get. When I get home I am marrying Carina and I am going to buy us a little cottage where we can live out our days."

"Not I, pal. I'm not getting weighed down with a wife until I am close to death and need someone to take care of me." Sven said.

"Boy, what a catch you will be," Hans replied and then he leaned back in the seat and closed his eyes to catch a little shut eye during the ride to Berlin.

Once Hans and Sven got to Berlin they found a hotel where they could stay while in the city. Hans asked Sven, "Do you want to share a room and save a little money?"

"No way," Sven said. "I want my own room. You never know when you're going to get lucky."

"Is that all you think about, women and booze?" Hans asked.

"Those are the two most important things in life, my friend. Without them, life just isn't worth living," Sven replied as he grabbed the keys to his room and walked away twirling the hotel key around his finger. Hans stood there with a look of disbelief on his face and said to himself, "Unbelievable, I can't believe I like that guy."

The next morning Hans woke up before sunrise, he wanted to get a head start on the day and wanted to make sure he had the whole day to do whatever he wanted to do. It was the first time Hans had any sort of freedom. It had been months since he had been let loose and he wanted to take advantage of every minute. The first stop was Brandenburger Tor (the Brandenburg Gate) it is one of Berlin's original city gates, erected in 1791.

It marked the entry to the Under den Linden Avenue as part of the boulevard that led to the royal seat of the Prussian monarchs. The monument is topped by a chariot driven by a winged goddess. The chariot and goddess were once taken to Paris by Napoleon as booty during the Napoleonic wars but was returned after the dictator's reign.

Hans was fumbling with his camera, tying to put some film in it in order to get a picture of the gate. The film did not want to cooperate and Hans looked as helpless as a child struggling with the camera. Hans heard a woman's voice from behind him. "I have one of those. Can I give you a hand?" Hans looks up in the direction from whence the voice came and came face to face with a very beautiful woman. "Please, that would be great," Hans said.

Hans handed the woman the camera and she had the film in it in seconds. "I feel like an idiot. Thank you, miss, I owe you one," Hans gratefully tells the woman.

"Okay, you can buy me a cup of coffee then?" the woman said.

Hans looked at the young woman in disbelief of what he had heard.

"Coffee, you owe me so I want some coffee."

Hans couldn't believe what he was hearing, a beautiful woman like her wanting to have coffee with him. Hans was spoken for man but he was not dead. Getting the chance to have coffee and talk to a pretty girl sounded like a wonderful way to spend lunch. "Sure, I would love to buy you a coffee," Hans said.

"Great, I know a wonderful café near here. It has a wonderful atmosphere, you will love it," the woman said.

Hans and the woman started walking to the café. Hans asks the woman, "What is your name?"

"Greta," she replied.

"Well, Greta, where are you from?" Hans asked trying to get the conversation going.

"I am from Vienna, I am here on holiday until Friday," Greta said.

"Really?" Hans said. "I am on leave until Friday as well."

At the café they talk about what they thought of Berlin so far. The sites they want to see while there and some of the history of the city.

Greta asks Hans, "Have you seen the Neue Reichskanzlei (the Reich's Chancellery) yet? It's a must see. Come with me tomorrow and see it with me. It will be fun and I hear this Chancellery is amazing. The Chancellery was built in 1938 and was the new Reich's Chancellery for Hitler's vision of a new Germany, it was very impressive with its long corridors and a quarry of red marble designed to make a person feel small."

Hans really didn't think much about Nazism or its ideology either or have any desire to see the Chancellery but he thought if he got the chance to spend the day with her, it was okay with him.

"Hey," Greta said. "We could also go see the Olympiastadion (Olympic Stadium). We will have a great day. The Stadium was built in 1936 for the Berlin Olympics. Hitler used it as a huge propaganda tool promoting the new Third Reich and the supremacy of the Aryan race."

To Hitler's chagrin, African-American Jesse Owens won four gold medals at the Berlin games beating the German master race in track. Hitler was infuriated of having black sub human, proving that the Germans were no Aryan supermen. Yet Hitler was still undaunted in his belief of the German supremacy.

CHAPTER FOUR

AT EIGHT THE NEXT morning Hans meets Greta in the lobby at his hotel. "Good morning, Greta, ready for an exciting day?" Hans asked.

"You bet, could hardly sleep last night," Greta said.

Hans grabbed her hand and said, "Let's go catch the bus to the Chancellery, it should be here very soon."

"Okay," Greta said.

They quickly walk out the lobby entryway and scurried to the bus stop a block away. Hans and Greta caught the bus at the stop and climbed aboard and found a seat in the middle of the bus.

As the bus drove down the road, the smell of the exhaust from the bus was getting stronger and stronger. By the time the bus got to the Chancellery Hans and Greta were feeling a little light-headed from the fumes of the exhaust. "Do you feel okay, Greta?" Hans asked.

"Feeling just a little woozy, how about you?" Greta asked.

"I feel like I have been out all night with my buddy Sven, just a little loopy."

"Let's go in the Chancellery, I can't wait to see it," Greta said.

There were red, black, and white swastika banners streaming from the top of the Chancellery, the largest banners Hans has ever seen. They walked inside and it took their breath away. It was beautiful and very intimidating at the same time. In the long hallway there were very large doors going into the Furor's reception hall. The doors were about seventeen feet high with a large "A" laid over an "H" standing for Adolf Hitler. Hans thought it was a bit gaudy and thought that Hitler must really be a bit self-absorbed. Greta was fascinated with the Chancellery and acted as if the place was a holy shrine. It was a side of Greta Hans had not seen and wasn't sure he liked.

Greta began to tell Hans about the Nazis and their ideology. Hans asked, "Greta, are you a Nazi?"

"Yes," Greta said. "Since 1934. I joined the Hitler Youth when I was fifteen and joined the Nazi party at eighteen." The Hitler Youth was like the boy or girl scouts except that they drilled Nazi ideology into the children and they were taught that they were the master race and that all other races were subhuman.

The girls also learn skills they needed to have to be a good German woman like sewing and cooking. Greta stood in front of Hans and said, "Hitler was sent to us by providence and is here to save Germany and the entire Aryan race. We will destroy the Bolsheviks and communists and one day will rule the world as the master race. Soon Europe will be Jew free and rid of all those traitors that stabbed Germany in the back and caused Germany to lose the war in WWI."

"Wow," Hans said feeling a little flabbergasted. Hans had friends back in Sweden that were Jewish and they were fine, hardworking, respectable individuals. Hans had no problem or reason to hate any Jews. He had joined the SS to fight communists not rid the world of Jews. The Jews seem to be okay to Hans. "They seem fine to me," Hans said. "I have never had a Jewish person do anything wrong to me."

"Jews are vermin, they are like rats. They invade your cities and breed like rats then spread disease and crime," Greta said to

Hans with a very serious look on her face. There was no doubt she was a Nazi from head to toe.

Hans felt a little put off by this. Hans was indoctrinated with that Nazi philosophy during SS training but he still didn't believe in their ideology and wasn't really sure he wanted to be with someone who felt that way. It was bad enough he had to deal with that in the SS but he wasn't sure he wanted that sort of thing in his private life. Hans and Greta continued on the tour of the Chancellery, when the tour was over they caught the bus to the Olympic Stadium.

Upon arrival to the stadium Hans and Greta got off of the bus and stood in amazement in front of the stadium. It was huge. The scale of the stadium was unbelievable. Hans thought to himself "Wow, there is nothing like this back home." Hans and Greta entered the stadium and walked from one end of the stadium to the other taking in all they were seeing and then went to the area where The Fuhrer had sat during the Olympic Games.

Greta sat in the seat where Hitler had sat during the Olympics. "Can you believe that I am actually sitting where our glorious Fuhrer sat, I just can't believe it, and this is like a dream," Greta said.

"Does it really excite you that much to sit where he has been?" Hans asked.

"Yes it does," Greta said. "Our Fuhrer is going to make this a better world for us, it's the greatest time in history and I have just touched part of it. Isn't it amazing?" Greta said like an excited little school girl. "Please take a picture for me. I want to show my friends at home, they won't believe it," Greta said.

Hans took Greta's camera from her and took her picture in the Fuhrer's seat. He couldn't believe someone would get so excited over sitting in a chair but Hans hadn't been brainwashed into idolizing Hitler and didn't quite understand the fascination that Greta had with him. "I think we need to head back to the hotel now, it's getting kind of late. I will take you to your hotel first, I don't want you to have to walk there alone at night it's just not safe," Hans said.

"Thank you, you're quite the gentleman," Greta said with a smile.

Once Hans and Greta reached her hotel they walked to her room. Greta fumbled for the key to unlock the door. "Ah, here it is," Greta said. "I thought I might have lost it." Greta stuck the key in the locked door but it wouldn't unlock. Greta wiggled the key and wrestled with the door but still could not get it unlocked.

"Let me try it," Hans said. Hans took the key from Greta and put the key in the lock, turned the key and the door opened without giving Hans any problem. Hans looked at Greta and smiled.

"Now I feel like a fool," Greta said.

"It just needed a man to show it who the boss is," Hans replied.

Greta rolled her eyes and stepped into her room. Greta turned around just inside the doorway. She slowly slid her hand up the edge of the door, blocking the door to keep Hans from entering with a slight tease. Greta seductively said, "Would you like to come in for a little night cap?"

"Thank you, Greta, I really appreciate the offer, I truly do but I can't," Hans said. "I have a girl waiting for me back home."

"Maybe so but she is in Sweden, you're in Berlin now," Greta said.

"You're a very beautiful woman, Greta. Even prettier than Carina, my girl back home, but beauty is only skin deep. A pretty face doesn't make a pretty heart and my Carina has a heart as big as a fjord. I couldn't hurt her. To tell you the truth any other man would be a fool not to come in but I just can't. I hope you can understand," Hans said sincerely.

"Tell Carina she got a good man, I hope I get as lucky as her," Greta said.

Hans leaned forward toward Greta and gave her a soft kiss on the cheek.

"Thanks for going with me today, I had a wonderful time. Good night," Hans said to Greta and turned to walk away.

"You don't know what you're missing," Greta said sarcastically.

Hans looked back at Greta while walking away, they smiled at each other and both waved goodbye. They each felt a since of sadness as Hans walked away. They enjoyed each other's company and had become close in the short time together but they both knew they would never see each other again.

Hans got back to the hotel and walked into the hotel lobby. "Sir, there is a message here for you," the clerk behind the counter said.

Hans took the message from the clerk and began to read it. "Effective immediately, all leave is canceled. Return to your training center for assignment to your unit." Hans rushed up to Sven's room to see if he was in so he could give him the news.

Hans got to Sven's room and knocked on the door, there was no answer. Hans then turns the handle to the door and the door opened. There Is Sven passed out on the bed with his head hanging over the side of the bed. Hans walked over to the bed and shook Sven trying to wake him up. "Sven, Sven!" Hans said loudly.

Sven raised his head a little and mumbled. "No, no, no, no don't take them off, I like it like that." Then Sven passed back out letting his head fall over the side of the bed again. Ten thirty in the evening and the guy was already plastered.

"Well, I guess this will have to wait till morning," Hans said. Hans was leaving Sven's room. Hans thought to himself that he had better leave the door unlocked so he will be able to get in the room and wake Sven in the morning. Hans planned to be up at five in the morning to make sure he had plenty of time to wake Sven and pull his drunken butt together and catch the first bus out of Berlin. As Hans was leaving the room and looked back at Sven and said sarcastically, "What would I do without you, buddy?"

Hans continued on to his room for a little sleep before the trip back to the training center in the morning. Hans wanted to get at least a few hours of sleep. Hans knew he would be taking care of Sven most of the day tomorrow, as usual after Sven having a night and day of drunken debauchery. The next morning Hans went to Sven's room to wake him. Hans shook Sven trying to wake him. Hans could smell Sven's breath, he smelled like a brewery. Hans continued to shake Sven but he would not awake. Hans spotted the pitcher for the wash basin on the dresser. He filled a glass of water from the pitcher and threw it in Sven's face. This woke Sven up immediately. Sven sat straight up and gasped for air. "What the hell did you do that for?" Sven asked, mad as a hornet.

"Get up, leave has been canceled and we have to get back to the training center to receive our orders immediately," Hans replied.

"Son of a bitch, just when I was starting to have a good time," Sven said.

"You call passing out from binge drinking fun?" Hans said.

"Maybe not, but a man has to get a little rest between women. I can't think of a better way to do it," Sven said.

"You have some serious issues, my friend. Get off your butt and get ready, we have a bus to catch," Hans said.

"Okay, okay, just give me a minute," Sven replied. "It will just take me five minutes and I will be ready to go."

CHAPTER FIVE

HANS AND SVEN CAUGHT the first bus out of Berlin just in time. Sven fell asleep about two minutes after he sat down in the bus and slept the whole trip back to the training center. Hans couldn't sleep. He kept wondering what could have possibly happened for them to cancel all leave. Hans thought whatever it is it must be important. Hans sat back in his seat and began gazing out the window watching the buildings of the city go by.

Hans said to himself, "Well, it was a short visit but I will have some good memories of Berlin at least." Hans wiggled and scrunched down in his seat trying to get comfortable for the ride back to the training center. It was going to be a long boring ride so Hans thought that he would try and get as comfortable as possible. Having to ride on a bus down a bumpy old road for hours wasn't going to be pleasant.

Once Hans and Sven had reached the training center, they headed straight for the headquarters building to receive their orders. Hans and Sven met the duty sergeant just inside the doors of the headquarters building. "We were called back from leave from Berlin to receive orders to our units, who do we to see?" Hans asked the sergeant. The sergeant said, "Hauptsturmfurer (Captain) Fryzel. Wait here and I will see if he can see you. What are your names?"

"Our names are Gruber and Eriksson, Sergeant," Hans replied.

The sergeant said, "Wait here." And he walked down the hall to the captain's door. The sergeant knocked on the door and from inside a voice said, "Enter." The sergeant went into the room. Hans couldn't hear anything they were saying but the sergeant soon came out and said, "Okay, come on back the captain will see you now." Hans and Sven walked down the hall and into the captain's office.

Hans said to the captain, "*Oberfusillires* (Privates) Gruber and Eriksson reporting for orders, Captain."

"Yes, we have been waiting for you, men," the captain said. "You will be reporting to *Obergruppenfuhrer* (General) Steiner of the Fifth SS Panzergrenadier Division Wiking. You will be sent to the unit tomorrow morning on the train. I can't tell you where you are going, that is classified but you will get briefed when you reach your destination. Any questions, men?"

"No, Captain," Hans and Sven replied.

"Very well, men," the captain said. "Go see the sergeant at the reception desk and he will square you away."

"Yes, sir, thank you, Captain," Hans replied.

Hans and Sven turned to leave the room. "Aren't you soldiers forgetting something?" asked the captain.

They turn to face the captain and Hans asked, "What would that be, Captain?" The captain raised his right arm up and gave a Nazi salute and said, "Heil Hitler."

Hans and Sven snapped their heels and raise their arms to return the salute and in unison yelled, "Heil Hitler!" Hans and Sven had both been through the Nazi indoctrination in SS training but still felt a little uneasy saluting and hailing Hitler. Hans and Sven had talked about it before. They had decided to go through the motions and play the part while they were serving in the SS, if that's what it took to go fight the Russians. It seemed like such a trivial thing they would have to do to get the opportunity to fight so they decided to play along. Little did they know that this was no game they were playing.

The next morning Hans and Sven arrived at the train station. The train was the longest train they had ever seen, it seemed to stretch to the horizon. There were tanks, artillery pieces, and hundreds of men on the train. They boarded the train to their new mystery destination, not knowing what the future had in store for them. They were both excited and fearful at the same time. Hans says to Sven, "Well, we are finally on our way, buddy."

Sven said, "I wonder how long it will take to get to where we are going."

"Don't know," Hans said. "Who knows, could be hours or it would be days."

The train slowly started rolling away from the station. It seemed to be straining under the weight of the load it was pulling. Hundreds of men and thousands of tons of military cargo all headed to the same place. "Must be a hell of a lot of excitement going to go somewhere," Hans thought to himself.

"They are really building up for something," Sven said. "Must be a new offensive somewhere, can't wait to get in to the mix of it."

Hans thought of the Winter War of 1939, fighting with the Finns against the Russians. Being a soldier is a hard life but something about the danger appealed to him. The horrors Hans experienced during the war still come back to haunt him in his dreams occasionally but something about war calls him back and gives him a desire to go back into battle.

After days on the train they finally reached their destination. "We are finally here," Sven said to Hans.

"Where is here?" Hans replied.

Sven said, "Let's go find out, you don't know until you ask." Hans and Sven got off of the train and spotted an SS soldier standing next to a motorcycle just outside of the train station. Hans asked the soldier, "Where would we find the headquarters to SS Wiking?"

"I am heading there now," the soldier said. "Hop on and I will give you a lift there."

"There is only the bike and a side car, which can only take one of us," Hans said.

"She can handle the both of you. If she can get me all the way across the Russian steps she can handle you boys. You, (pointing to Sven) get in the sidecar. You, (pointing at Hans) get on the back behind me." Hans and Sven climbed on the bike and held on. "Here we go boys, don't fall off. I'm not going to stop and pick you back up if you do. There are still Russian snipers between here and there and I am not going to get a bullet in the head for some green recruit," the soldier said then turned the throttle on the bike and they rolled away down the dirt road toward the SS headquarters. Once they arrived at the SS headquarters Hans and Sven walk right in, they were both excited in anticipation of getting to their new unit.

As they walked through the entry door to the building they run face to face into SS *Obergrumppenfuhrer* (General) Felix Steiner. Steiner was almost a legion in the SS and was widely known and admired as a battle-winning general. His skills as a master military strategist had been tested time and time again with victory after victory to his name. It was an honor to get to meet him and they were both in awe of his presence.

"General, I am Gruber and this is Eriksson, we are reporting for duty," Hans said in a waving tone that sounded like a teenage boy going through puberty.

"Well that's wonderful, welcome, boys, we can always use more good men."

"Thank you, General," Hans said.

"Sergeant," the general bellowed to the duty sergeant. Show these new recruits to their units."

"Yes, General, right away," the sergeant replied then the he motioned with his arm for Hans and Sven to follow him.

The men walked out of the headquarters building and down the dirt road about a quarter of a mile. Standing in front of a long row of tents stood platoon Sergeant Heidi. Heidi was a tuff and gruff looking man, a soldier's solder. He looked as if he had been to hell and back and the scars on his face reinforced that theory. "Sergeant Heidi," said the sergeant who brought Hans and Sven there to meet Heidi. "These are your new recruits, Gruber and Eriksson. Fresh from the farm and they are all yours." The sergeant who had brought them said with a snicker.

"Thanks," Heidi replied. "More cannon fodder."

"You men take the last tent in the row. The men who put it up won't need it any longer." Hans and Sven just looked at each other, they wasn't really sure if the men who had the tent before went home or were dead. Hans said, "Thanks, Sergeant." Then they both headed for the tent.

"There will be a briefing at seventeen hundred in front of the tents, make sure your asses are there," Heidi said.

"Yes, Sergeant," they both replied and continued to the tent. Hans and Sven were both glad to finally get to their unit but still had no idea where they were. Hans was sure they would soon find out at the briefing.

Just before seventeen hundred Hans and Sven were at the briefing site with the other men of the unit. No one at the briefing wanted to talk to Hans or Sven, they seemed to intentionally steer themselves away from them. Hans spotted an *obergefreiter* (corporal) that looked like he might be friendly and that Hans might be able to talk to without being brushed away. Hans walked up to the corporal and said. "Hi, Corporal, how are you doing today?"

The corporal looked at Hans for a couple of seconds and said, "I am doing fine, thank you, how are you?"

"Great, thanks," Hans replied.

"Can you answer a question for me?" Hans asked.

"Sure, kid, what is it?" the corporal said.

"How come no one seems to want to talk to us, it's like we have the plague or something?" Hans asked the corporal.

"It's nothing personal, recruit," the corporal said. "The old timers don't want to get to know the replacements. The replacements tend to get themselves killed because they have no combat experience. They tend to do foolish things and end up dead before they can learn how to keep themselves alive. The guys who have been here awhile don't want to be around them because their stupidity may get them killed as well."

"I can understand that," Hans said. We were with the Finns in '39 fighting the Russians."

"Oh, that's good," the corporal said. "At least you have some experience with combat."

"What's your name, Corporal?" Hans asked.

"I'm Fritz Olam," the corporal said. "What are your names?"

"I am Hans Gruber and this is Sven Eriksson," Hans said. "We are Swedish volunteers."

"It's nice to meet the both of you," Fritz said. "Swedes, don't see many of you guys in the SS. Don't worry, boys, the others will warm up to you once you show them what you're made of. From what I have heard, looks like you two will get the chance to do that very soon."

Sergeant Heidi showed up at the briefing at seventeen hundred on the dot. Hans could tell right away Heidi was a stickler for punctuality. "Hello, men," Heidi said. "I have some news from command that we will be heading out tomorrow. We are moving out to Rostov-on-Don in the Caucasus. This assault will be called Operation Maus. Our mission is to secure the oil fields. This oil field is vital to Army Group South's offensive called Operation Case Blue. The purpose of this operation is to capture Stalingrad and the Baku oil fields. We have a big job ahead of us, men, Rostove and the entire Don region has to be recaptured. We head out at zero six hundred. Be in formation and ready to move out."

CHAPTER SIX

"The Caucasus," Sven said. "No wonder it took so long to get here, we're halfway around the world."

"We're not halfway around the world, you idiot," Hans said to Sven. "We are just half way through Russia. Look at it this way, Sven, the job is half done. Once we capture Stalingrad and Moscow the war will be over. Look, we will kill us a few Russians and be home for Christmas," Hans said.

"You're probably right," Sven replied. "Probably won't even get the barrel of my rifle warm before we go home. Let's go see if we can get us some chow, I'm starving."

"Me too," Hans said. "We haven't eaten since yesterday, I feel like my stomach is eating me from the inside out."

"Well then we better go find us something to eat," Sven said. "Come on, let's go."

Hans and Sven found the *feldkuchen* (field kitchen) and went in to get something to eat. The kitchen was serving *graubrot* (gray rye bread) and *fleish* (a tinned meat). There were also a few vegetables and a little butter for the bread.

Hans tasted the tinned meat and immediately made a sour face. "Boy, this sure isn't home cooking, that's for sure," Hans said disgusted with the taste of the food.

"Don't be a baby, it can't be that bad," Sven said. Sven took a bite of the meat and said. "It doesn't taste that bad to me, I don't see what you're complaining about."

"I don't doubt it, Sven, you would eat a cat that's been run over in the road," Hans replied.

"A man has got to eat," Sven said. "You need to learn not to be so picky." This will probably seem like a feast compared to what we will get in the field."

"You're probably right," Hans said. "Let's get done with this and go get some sleep, I have a feeling tomorrow is going to be a long day."

Hans woke up at zero five hundred. Looking at his watch Hans was thinking that he had a whole hour to leisurely get ready for the zero six hundred company formation. Hans had to piss something terrible. Hans said, "Oh dear god, my teeth are floating. I have to piss something fierce." Hans flipped the flap of the tent and walked outside to relieve himself. Hans looked up to see where he was going and was shocked at what he saw. There were Panzer tanks and half-track troop carriers lined up on the road outside of their tents about a mile long. Hans yelled, "Sven! Get your ass up and come take a look at this!"

Sven said, "All right, all right just give me a second." Sven stuck his head out of the tent and saw the line of vehicles. "Holy crap! Where did those come from?" he asked.

"Did you hear them come in last night?" Hans asked Sven.

"No, Hans, I didn't hear a thing."

"Neither did I," Hans said. "We must have really been out of it last night."

"Yeah," Sven said. "I wonder what was in that tinned meat we ate last night."

"I don't know," Hans replied. "Whatever it was, it sure put us out. I think I am about to piss my pants, I've got to go,"

Hans said and quickly ran behind the tent to relieve himself and began to urinate.

Hans kept going and going and going and it didn't sound like it was going to stop. Sven yells back to Hans, "Dear god! It sounds like a horse pissing back there, how much water did you have before we sacked out?"

"I don't know but apparently it was a lot," Hans said. "Ah, what a relief I feel much better." Hans finish the task at hand and went back in the tent to put on his uniform and grab his gear. Hans wanted to make sure he was not late for formation.

At zero six hundred all the men of the unit were lined up in front of the tents. Sergeant Heidi showed up right on time. Heidi stood in front of the men and yelled, "Attention!" The whole unit snapped to attention at his command. Heidi then addressed the men, "We have a big job ahead of us, men, and many of you will not make it back. You can be assured that our great nation and the Fuhrer will be grateful for your sacrifice to protect the fatherland." Heidi then raised his hand in a traditional Nazi salute and shouted, "Heil Hitler!" The entire unit raised their hands to return the salute and in unison shouted, "Heil Hitler!"

"Now, get your asses on the half-tracks!" Heidi bellowed. The entire unit scurried to the half-tracks and climbed aboard. Sven said to Hans, "We are finally going to the front. We are finally going to get the chance to kill some of those Russian bastards."

"Don't get too cocky, Sven, remember, they will be shooting back," Hans said reminding Sven of the true danger they were about to experience.

"Don't you worry about me, Hans," Sven said. "I am too pretty to get killed." Hans and Sven just smiled at each other as the half-track began to pull away. They were finally on their way.

The column Hans and Sven were riding in was a half mile away from the town of Rostov. Hans was sitting in the half-track thinking of writing a letter to Carina back home and piecing together what he wanted to say to her in his mind. Hans stood up in the half-track to stretch his legs, they have been traveling for quite a while and Hans's back was hurting from sitting so long. Hans looked over the front of the half-track to see where they were going and looking at all the vehicles in front of him.

The half-track in front of Hans's suddenly explodes. Shrapnel, fire, and body parts fly everywhere. Part of a leg from the knee down lands in the middle of the half-track Hans and Sven were in. The driver of the half-track slams on the brakes, jumps out of the vehicle and dives into the ditch at the side of the road. The men in the back of the half-track soon followed the driver including Hans and Sven into the ditch. Explosions began all around the men in every direction.

It was a Russian artillery barrage. Their forward observers had discovered the SS column and radioed back for artillery support. The Russians had opened up on the column with 152 mm Howitzers in an attempt to destroy the column before they reached the city. Five of the SS's Panzer tanks made it to the top of a ridge and spotted the artillery emplacements. The Panzers open fired on the Russian artillery and with ten tank rounds eliminated the Russian threat.

The Russians knew the SS was there so there was no chance of catching the Russians with their pants down with a surprise attack. The unit commander ordered the men to dig in for the night and prepare for a frontal attack in the morning. Hans, Sven, and the rest of the men in the unit dug in for the night. The men dug foxholes with their shovels just big enough for two men to squat down out of sight of any enemy that would possibly attack during the night.

There was about a half hour of sunlight left before the sun went down. Hans thought it would be a good opportunity to write Carina and let her know that he and Sven had made it to their duty stations and how to contact him when she would write a letter. Hans reached into his upper breast pocket and pulled out a small pencil and some paper he had stashed in his pocket back at the training center. Sitting in a small foxhole with his knees in his chest and rifle to his side, Hans began to write a letter to Carina, the best he could give the circumstances.

Hans propped the paper against his leg and began to write.

To my sweet Carina,

I am sorry I haven't written you sooner but I wanted to wait until I had reached my duty station so I could tell you where to send the letter when you write me, that is, if you haven't replaced me already. You can address your letter to the Fifth SS Panzer Division, Wiking and the letter will reach me. I can't tell you where I am unfortunately due to the location being classified. I can tell you that where I am is very beautiful and the accommodations provided are very comfortable. It's a bit boring though. All we seem to do is drill, drill, drill, march, march, march so there is no reason to worry for me, I am far from danger.

Oh well, that's the life of a soldier. I miss you so much. I miss the sound of your voice and the way you gracefully float across the floor when you are walking. How do you do that by the way? Please write me a letter soon, I can't wait to hear from you and to get an update of what is all going on at home. Tell momma I said hi and that I love her very much. Also, tell her I will write her as soon as I can. Carina, I have thought about it and I want to marry you the next time I come home

on leave. I know it's a lot sooner than you expected but it's
something I would really like to do.

I hope you agree, sweetheart, it really means a lot to
me. Besides, I will receive more pay for being married and I
could send more back home. It's a win-win for you. You get a
handsome, intelligent, and wonderful guy like me and more
money. What more could a woman want? Well my love, I
must go for now. I love you with all my heart and I can't wait
to get home and make you my wife. Write soon.

Love always and forever,
Hans

Hans put the pencil and paper in his pocket. Hans started daydreaming about Carina and how the wedding would be and slowly drifted off to sleep.

The next morning Hans wakes up to Sven hitting him in the head on the top of his helmet with the butt of Sven's rifle. "Wake up, sweetheart, it's time to move out," Sven said as he climbed out of the foxhole.

Hans slowly woke from his slumber and raise his hands to rub his face. "Oh shit," Hans said with a bit of urgency in his voice. "We have to get to the morning briefing for our orders." Hans pulled himself out of the foxhole and they both ran to the half-track they were assigned to and waited for Sergeant Heidi to come and brief them on today's attack plan.

Heidi walks up to Hans, Sven, and the rest of their squad waiting at the half-track. "All right boys, listen up," Heidi said. "We are going to attack Rostove. The Russians have the town well-fortified with men and small artillery. There is also a battalion strength tank regiment guarding the city as far as we can tell. Your squad's mission is to follow that Panzer in front of this half-track in support of the tank into the city. Remember boys, men are replaceable but tanks are hard to come by, don't screw up," Heidi said with a bit of a snarl on his face. "Anyone have questions?"

"No, Sergeant!" the squad said in unison.

"All right, prepare to move out," Heidi said. Heidi walked on down the road to give the next squad their orders.

"Boy, he's a loving and caring guy, isn't he," Sven said with a hint of sarcasm in his voice.

"Yes, his momma must be very proud," Hans replied.

The squad gathered behind their assigned Panzers and readied themselves for the assault. "Move out!" Someone in front of their tank yelled. The tanks began to roll with each squad closely following behind. About a hundred feet in front of the column, the trees ended and gave way to a large clearing. It was a wheat field about a quarter mile from the city. To the left and to the right of the unit, the fields extended to the horizon. There was no place for cover to protect the men while they assaulted the city from Russian machine gun fire except for the little cover the tanks provided.

CHAPTER SEVEN

FROM ACROSS THE FIELD Hans could see them. There were hundreds of Russian men and many T-34 tanks barreling across the field toward Hans's unit. The tank Hans was following suddenly stopped. The tank took aim at one of the enemies' T-34's and fired. The Russian T-34 exploded throwing its turret one hundred feet in the air before falling to the ground crushing an unsuspecting Russian soldier.

Just before both side reached the center of the field Hans raised his rifle and took aim at a Russian soldier running directly toward him. Hans could see the Russian's face and it was a face of a boy, he couldn't have been over seventeen. He hesitated for a moment and thought how the soldier reminded him of a young boy that lived near him back home. Hans wondered how the young soldier's mother would take the news of her son's death and felt a little sad for her.

There was an explosion near Hans that jolted him back to reality. He resumed his aim at the boy and fired his rifle. The round hit the young soldier in the head going through his helmet and into his brain. The boy's head was violently thrown back when the round struck him and he fell to the ground. The young man was dead before he even hit the dirt.

Once the SS and Russians met in the center of the field the chaos began. Both armies began fighting in hand to hand combat, men and tanks were scattered everywhere. Tanks were running over their own men maneuvering around to either avoid getting hit or to get into a good position to fire upon the enemy tanks. There were explosions everywhere and bullets were flying from every direction. The fields had caught fire from the exploding shells and smoke began to obstruct the view of every soldier on the field.

Hans turned his head to look behind so he could see if Sven was following behind but Hans could not see him. He turned back around to face the enemy and just caught a glimpse of a Russian soldier running toward him. Before Hans could even react to the danger that was approaching him, the Russian hit Hans in the face with the butt of his rifle knocking Hans unconscious and he fell to the ground. Sven saw Hans go down and quickly ran over to save him.

Sven thrusted his bayonet into the chest of the Russian soldier and the soldier gave out a gasp. Sven tried to pull the bayonet out of the Russian's chest but it would not come out. The bayonet got stuck in the soldier's ribs. Sven pulled and twisted the bayonet trying to free it while the Russian soldier was screaming in shock and pain. Sven then fired his rifle into the Russian's chest freeing the bayonet.

The Russian took a step back from the force of the shell entering his body. Then the Russian soldier's eyes grew wide open as in disbelief of what was happening then fell to the ground dead. Sven bent down to see if Hans was still alive. There was a little blood over his left eye and his nose was bleeding but he was still breathing.

Sven said, "You're going to be okay, buddy. You're just going to have a hell of a headache when you wake up." Sven knew he couldn't stay with Hans to take care of him, it made Sven too much of an easy target for the Russians. Sven stood up over Hans and smiled. "What a way to get out of doing your job," Sven said then turned and quickly run off to join his squad in battle.

Hans came too just as the battle begins to die down to a young Russian soldier slapping him in the face to bring him out of his slumber. Hans saw the soldier and immediately thought to himself that today was going to be the last day of his life. The Russians rarely take Waffen-SS prisoners. The normal Russian procedure is to put a bullet in the back of the head of any captured SS soldier. The young Russian soldier grabs Hans by the coat with both hands and shakes him. "You must take me prisoner," the Russian soldier said.

"Okay, okay," Hans said just a little shocked at the request. "I will take you prisoner." The Russian soldier pulls Hans to his feet then reaches down to pick up Hans's rifle and hands the rifle to him. Hans slings his rifle over his left shoulder and puts his right arm on the shoulders of the Russian.

The Russian helps Hans keep his balance and helps him walk back to the German lines. While walking back to the lines Hans asked the Russian soldier, "What is your name?"

"My name is Borya, what is yours?" the soldier said.

"Hans. Why do you want to be taken prisoner, Borya?" Hans asks.

"I am a cook not a communist," Borya said. "The party forced me to become a soldier. They ordered us to fight to death if necessary to stop the Germans and if any of us retreated they would be shot on sight."

"I'm not a Nazi and you're not a communist. Just goes to show, you never know what the fickle finger of fate has in stored for you," Hans said with amusement. When Hans and Borya made it back to the German lines, Hans reported to Sergeant Heidi to find out what to do with his new prisoner. Hans told Heidi everything that Borya had told him. "Being a private and a cook as well, your Russian prisoner is worthless for getting any strategic information. Get rid of him," Heidi said without any reservations and turned to walk away.

"Wait, Sergeant," Hans said quickly. "The prisoner is a cook. Can't we use him to serve the men?"

"Yes," Heidi said. "That is a good idea, it will free up another soldier to fight. Take the prisoner to the sergeant at the chow hall and turn the prisoner over to him."

"Yes, Sergeant," Hans replied then turned, grabbed Borya by the arm and began to escort him to the chow hall.

The tent where they prepared and served the troops' chow was about a quarter mile away from the front lines. While walking, Borya said, "Thank you for saving me, Hans. I was worried that the sergeant would order you to shoot me. I have heard before that the SS doesn't take prisoners."

"Don't worry," Hans told Borya. "As long as you do what you are told and don't cause any trouble you have nothing to worry about."

"Are we friends?" Borya asked Hans.

"Yes," Hans replied trying to calm Borya's nerves. "Remember, just do what you are told and you will be okay. I will try and check on you if I can but I am no baby sitter, I am a soldier and I have a job to do."

"Thank you," Borya said, feeling a little better about the situation he was in. Hans and Borya reach the chow tent and found the sergeant in charge. "Sergeant, this is Borya," Hans said to the sergeant. "I took him prisoner this afternoon."

"Yeah, so what does that have to do with me?" the sergeant replied.

"I asked my platoon sergeant what to do with him and he told me to bring him to you," Hans said.

"Why the hell would I want some communist bastard in my kitchen?" the sergeant asked with a growl.

"Borya's not a communist. He was a conscript and forced to fight, he hates the communists. Besides, he has experience as a cook and would free up one of our men to fight."

"Well, okay," the sergeant said reluctantly. "If he gives me any trouble, any trouble at all I will take him out back and shoot him myself."

"I don't think he will give you any trouble, Sergeant. I think he is a good man." Hans said. "I don't know how any Russian can be a good man. They are all murderers and rapists," the sergeant mumbled.

"Give him a chance, Sergeant, I think I will do a good job for you," Hans said. Hans turned to Borya with a smile on his face and said, "Good luck, comrade, better be a good boy."

Borya quickly grabbed Hans's hand with both of his hands and said to him, "Thank you, my friend, I will never forget this." Hans smiled, gave Borya a wink and left Borya to return to the front.

Hans returned to the front lines and found the foxhole he and Sven had dug the previous day but Sven was not there. Hans wondered if Sven had survived the battle or if he had lost his best friend. Not knowing what had happened to Sven or even where his body may be made Hans both worried and depressed. Hans questioned his logic in asking his best friend to join him in enlisting in the German Army where he could get himself killed.

Hans knew that Sven wasn't the most levelheaded guy and that it would be very possible that Sven would get himself killed doing something foolish if he didn't keep an eye on him. Hans heard someone approaching and turned to see who it was. It was Sergeant Heidi headed his way with a scowl on his face you could see a mile away. Heidi had one of those faces only a mother could love and with the scowl on his face he looked even less appealing. "We are attacking again in the morning, zero six hundred," Heidi said to Hans.

"Have you seen Sven?" Hans asked.

"No, he didn't show up when we regrouped, he is MIA (Missing in action)," Heidi told Hans. "Make damn sure you're ready to go at zero six hundred," Heidi growled.

"I love you too, Sergeant," Hans replied. Heidi smiled at Hans then rushed off to the next foxhole to brief the other men.

It was beginning to rain and the temperature was dropping. Hans squatted down in the foxhole and got as comfortable as he could for the night then slowly drifted off to sleep. The next morning at zero five hundred Hans woke but he couldn't move. The temperature had dropped below freezing during the night and the rainwater had frozen. Hans couldn't believe it, he was frozen to the side of the foxhole and could not break free. Hans started yelling for help over and over for ten minutes. Finally someone came to the foxhole to free him. It was Sven.

"Sven, you're alive!" Hans said gratefully.

"Yes, I'm alive," Sven said. "What are you whining about?"

"I am frozen to the foxhole and can't get out," Hans said.

"Good god," Sven said sarcastically. "I leave for one evening and come home and you get yourself in trouble."

"Okay funny guy, just give me a hand and get me out of this," Hans said. Sven climbed in the hole and grabbed Hans's hands and gave a hard pull. Hans broke free from the foxhole and stood up. Hans doubled up his fist and hit Sven hard in the chest. *"Oooh!"* Sven moaned. "What the hell did you do that for?"

"Don't ever disappear on me like that again. I thought you were dead."

"I told you before dumbass, they are never going to get me. I am too pretty to die," Sven said with a grin. "Just stay behind me and you will be okay too."

Hans playfully shoved Sven and said, "You're an idiot."

"Let's go see if we can get something to eat before we have to go, I am starving. Those Russian women kept me up all night and I have worked up quite an appetite," Sven said with a snicker.

"If any Russian woman saw you they would shoot you on sight, they probably know your reputation all the way to Moscow," Hans said. "Come on, Romeo, let's get something to eat."

CHAPTER EIGHT

AT ZERO SIX HUNDRED the unit began to move out. Hans and Sven along with the other survivors of their squad crouch behind a Panzer tank and move toward the Russian lines. Five hundred yards from the Russian lines, the Russian artillery opens up on the SS. Hans and Sven try to take cover behind the Panzer but there is no safe place on the battlefield to take cover from the Russian barrage.

The Panzer to the left of Hans receives a direct hit from the artillery and explodes in a huge fireball. The explosion was so close it blew Hans and the rest of his squad to the ground. The Panzer Hans's squad was following continued to move forward toward the enemy leaving the squad completely without cover from enemy fire. Hans and his squad members slowly shake off the blow they received from the tank exploding and begin to run toward the Panzer they were previously escorting.

Before the squad could catch up to the tank it exploded throwing the whole squad to the ground again. One of Hans's squad members was hit with shrapnel through the throat. A two-inch piece of steel ripped through the neck of a young private just below the Adam's apple. The young man was convulsing, coughing, and choking on his own blood. Hans could tell the boy was going to die a slow and agonizing death and there was nothing he could do to help him.

Hans knelt down beside the boy and put his hand on the young soldier's cheek in the attempt to calm him. Hans said to the boy, "Close your eyes and think of home." The young soldier closed his eyes and Hans pulled his pistol out of his holster. Hans put the gun to the boy's head and pulled the trigger, it was the most humane thing Hans could do. Hans looked at the boy and tears began to swell up in his eyes, he looked so young. Hans wiped his eyes with his hands then quickly stood up and run to join the fight with his men.

The artillery barrage suddenly came to a close and there was a strange silence and calmness on the field. Hans's ears were ringing from the explosions of the artillery rounds but he could just make out the sounds of engines from across the field. It was the sounds from the engines of a dozen T-34 tanks screaming toward him from across the field. The Panzers open fire on the T-34 and immediately knock out two of the T-34s.

Twelve more T-34s suddenly appeared behind the first group and opens fire on the Panzers. It then became a slugging match between the Russian T-34s and the Waffen-SS's Panzer tanks. Russian ground troops began to form a defensive line behind the T-34s and opened fire on the SS infantry pinning them down halting the assault. Hans grabbed a Panzerfaust. A Panzerfaust is a German infantryman's antitank weapon. It is lightweight, powerful, and extremely effective.

Hans low crawled within range of the Panzerfaust's effective range and lined his sites on a T-34. Hans fired his weapon at the T-34 and made a direct hit, knocking off the tracks of the tank and completely destroying its capability to continue the fight. Hans low crawled back to the German lines and grabbed a second Panzerfaust.

Again Hans low crawled within range of another T-34 and fired the anti-tank weapon at the T-34. The round went through the turret of the tank killing all the crewmen inside. Hans again low crawled back to the German lines and grabbed another Panzerfaust. Hans did this again and again destroying five T-34s by himself. By late afternoon the battle was a stalemate, the Russians had held off yet another attack from the SS.

The SS once again made a strategic withdraw to regroup and rearm. During the withdraw Sven caught up with Hans while walking back to the assembly area. Sven said to Hans, "You're a hero, buddy. They will give you a medal for what you did today."

"I don't deserve a medal," Hans said. "I was just trying to save my own ass out there."

"You know, your mother would kill you if she knew you did that," Sven said to Hans. "I don't plan on telling her and you better not either or you will wind up like those tanks out there," Hans said. Sven slapped Hans on the back of the helmet and said, "Okay tough guy, let's go get something to eat I am starving."

"You're always hungry," Hans said.

"I am still a growing boy," Sven replied.

"Okay, Sven, let's go feed the beast." Hans and Sven made it to the mess tent and got themselves something to eat. As usual Hans did not like the food, it tasted like it was old and spoiled to him. Sven, on the other hand, gobbled up his food like a hungry dog, including licking his tray to get every morsel. "God, you are a pig, Sven," Hans said with a bit of distain.

"Isn't that the way you like them, big and dirty?" Sven replied.

"Are you saying my Carina is a big dirty pig? I will bust you in the mouth!"

"No," Sven said. "She is the exception to the rule."

"You are an asshole, Sven, why do I like you?"

"That's because you love me. You love me, you love me," Sven said teasingly with a musical tune.

"Ugh, let's go. We need to get back to our little home in the dirt," Hans said to Sven with a hint of frustration in his voice.

Outside the tent Hans notices a line of ten Russian soldiers. "Hold up, Sven," Hans said. "What's going on over there?"

"I don't know," Sven replied. Go ask that corporal in charge of them." Hans walked over to the corporal and he noticed Borya in the line of men. "What's going on here, Corporal?" Hans asked.

"We have been ordered by command not to take any prisoners. These Russian scums are to be shot," the corporal said.

Hans was shocked by this. He had to think of something quick or Borya would surely be killed. "I need one of these pigs to dig a trench for my captain, give me the ugly one at the end of the line I think he will do." Hans pointed at Borya.

"Go ahead, what do I care. We are going to take care of the whole dirty lot of them eventually, might as well get some work out of these worthless pigs," the corporal said.

Hans grabbed Borya by the arm, jerked him out of the line and said, "You're coming with me. I have something special in store for you, you Russian dog. Let's go."

Hans pushed Borya in front of him and pointed his rifle at Borya's back. Hans poked Borya in the back with his rifle and said, "Move you pig, I have a little work for you to do." With a rifle in his back Borya lead the way back to Hans and Sven's foxhole. Along the way Sven asked Hans, "Okay, Hans, now we are out of ear range, what's going on in that head of yours? Whatever it is I have a bad feeling about it."

Hans said, "Don't worry about it. You don't have to be involved."

"Do I even want to know?" Sven asked.

"You probably don't," Hans said. "I am going to let him go."

"Are you out of your mind? If they find out you did this they will shoot you," Sven said.

"I have to do this, Sven. He is not a communist and we are not Nazis. He surrendered to me to get away from the communists because he feared for his life, but if he stays here he will surely be shot. I think he stands a better chance back with the Russians."

"So, you're just going to let him go?" Sven asked.

"Yes," Hans replied. "You don't have to be involved with this. It is just something I have to do."

"Okay my friend. It's your head," Sven said. Hans waited for nightfall to execute the escape. He wanted to make sure there was as little of a chance as possible not to be discovered. At 1:00 a.m. Hans and Borya began their escape. Hans lead the way in a low crawl across no man's land in between the Russian and German lines in an effort to get Borya as close to the Russian lines as possible without getting either one of them killed.

The two made it halfway across the field when Hans said in a whisper, "You're on your own from here Borya, good luck."

"Thank you, Hans, you have saved my life three times now. I will never forget you. You are truly a friend."

"If we are still alive after the war you can buy me a beer," Hans said jokingly.

Borya grasped Hans's hand and squeezed it firmly in affection then crawled away into the night. Hans lay there on the ground and watched Borya crawl toward the Russian line hoping he makes it and survives the war.

Hans had low crawled back to the German lines as quietly as he could so he would not be discovered. Hans got within thirty feet of his foxhole and stood up thinking he was at a safe point back at the German line. A shot rings out and Hans is hit by a bullet one inch away from where he was shot in the

Winter War of '39. A young German sentry had spotted Hans walking in the night in front of the lines. Thinking Hans was a Russian on a reconnaissance patrol the soldier fired at him without finding out if he was friend or foe.

Four German SS men ran out to see if the enemy the young soldier shot was still alive, hoping to gather some information from him. The men got to Hans and discovered that he was SS as well. The soldiers quickly grabbed him and carried him back to the German line. Hans blacked out somewhere along the way. Hans came to in a makeshift hospital in a small town the Germans had captured during the invasion. The building was originally used by senior communist officials but had been taken over by the Germans and used as a hospital out of necessity.

It felt like luxury to Hans to be lying in clean white linen sheets. The staff was mainly Norwegian and there were even female nurses, it almost felt like being back at home. A nurse walks into the room and came directly to Hans's bed. "Hans Gruber?" the nurse asked.

"Yes, I am Hans."

"I have a letter for you. It smells like lilac, must be from someone special," the nurse said with a smile. The nurse handed Hans the letter and he immediately smells the envelope. It smelled just like Carina and Hans couldn't wait to read what she had sent him. Hans eagerly opens the envelope to read the letter and smells the paper one more time before he reads it.

My darling Hans,

First I want to tell you that I love you and I miss you terribly. My life feels so empty without you and sometimes I feel I can't go on without you. I think the only thing that keeps me going is the thought that when you come home we will finally be married. Please come home soon. Hans, I know you're not just drilling and marching around all day. We get the paper here too and they cover the war. I know your unit is in the thick of it and things are not going so well. I worry terribly about you but please don't lie to me anymore. The lies hurt worse than the pain of worrying about you.

Hans, I hate to tell you this but I have some terrible news. Your mother passed away last month. She had caught pneumonia and had gotten very ill. My mother had been taking care of her and was there when she passed. She died peacefully in her sleep and my mother and father took care of the funeral. She was like family to us and will be missed immensely. I am taking care of your mother's home until you return.

I am so sorry, Hans. She was a kind and caring woman and we all loved her very much. Come home soon, my love, I am waiting for you.

I will love you always and forever.

Carina

Hans put down the letter and began to quietly cry. He tried to be a man about it and not let his feelings show but he could not hold back the tears. Tears rolled down his cheeks but he did not make a sound, he didn't want the other men to think he was weak. An SS soldier does not cry.

CHAPTER NINE

HANS WAS AWARDED THE Iron Cross 2nd Class and promoted to corporal for single-handedly destroying five Russian T-34 tanks and given leave to go back home to recuperate from his wound. Hans was determined to take advantage of his leave and finally marry Carina. Hans boarded a train heading west to Germany. He would have to take several different trains to get to the German coast. It was an exhausting trip but once he had made it to the coast it was just a short ferry ride from Rostock, Germany to Trelleborg, Sweden then a short trip home to Osby.

Hans boarded the ferry in Rostock and the ferry soon began underway. He was almost home and he couldn't wait to see Carina. He hadn't told her that he was coming, he wanted to surprise her. "Oh crap," Hans said anxiously. He had forgotten to get a gift for Carina. Hans wanted to get her a souvenir or some type of gift from Germany but had forgotten due to being so excited to get home. "Oh well," Hans thought to himself. "Hopefully I will be enough. I guess I can always get her something from Germany next time I go on leave."

Hans felt a little disappointed with him but the feeling soon faded away as he began to think about going home again. Just before the ferry reached Swedish waters a German patrol boat pulled alongside the ferry and demanded the ferry to stop to be boarded and searched. The ferry captain complied and the German sailors boarded the ferry for a routine search for contraband, Jews, and deserters. One of the sailors walked up to Hans and said, "I need your papers, please." Hans handed the sailor his SS identification and his leave orders permitting him to travel to Sweden.

"What business do you have in Sweden?" the sailor asked.

"I'm Swedish, that's where I am from. I am going home to marry my girl," Hans told the sailor with a smile.

"Very nice, good luck, Swede," the sailor said. By the way, what the hell is a Swede doing in the SS? I didn't think you boys liked to fight."

"That's not true," Hans said. "Some of us love to fight," Hans raised his arm and made a fist in front of the sailor's face and said, "Want to see?"

"I can't right now, Swede," the sailor said with a little chuckle. "I'm too busy today, maybe next time."

The sailor handed Hans back his papers and said, "Good luck, Swede, if you're getting married you're going to need it. Women are more dangerous than the Russians."

"Not my Carina," Hans said. "She is as sweet as honey."

"Right," the sailor said with a smirk. The sailor put has hand on Hans's shoulder and gave it a light shake and said, "Give it a couple of years, pal, you'll see." The sailor then turned and walked away, carrying on with the job at hand. The sailors completed their search and released the ferry to continue on to Sweden. Hans could hardly contain himself, he was almost home, just a few more miles to Trelleborg.

The Ferry reached Trelleborg and docked at the port. Hans had made it to Sweden but now had to figure out how to get home to Osby. He spotted a warehouse where they loaded trucks with the cargo from the ships that come to port and thought that the warehouse might be a good place to catch a ride home with one of the trucks heading north. Hans walked to the warehouse and found the warehouse foreman belting out orders to the men loading the trucks.

The foreman was a middle-aged man that looked like he had never had a good time in his whole life and his demeanor reflected that assumption. "Excuse me, sir," Hans said to the foreman.

"What do you want boy, can't you see I'm busy?" the foreman said.

"Yes, sir, I am sorry to bother you but I need to get to Osby and I was wondering if I might catch a ride with one of the trucks headed north?" Hans asked.

"Good lord," the foreman said. Does this look like some kind of bus station to you?"

"No, sir," Hans replied.

"You people are a pain in the ass," the foreman grumbled to himself. There was a group of truck drivers sitting at the table playing cards while waiting for their trucks to be loaded. The foreman bellowed to the truckers, "Hey, any of you high rollers going north through Osby?"

"Yes, I am, why?" One of the truckers replied.

"This boy needs to get to Osby, think you can give him a lift?" the foreman asked.

"I sure can, it will be nice to have a little company for a change," the trucker said.

The trucker was a little old gray-haired man in his middle 60s at least. The man had a tiny stature, didn't even look tall enough to see over the steering wheel. Hans looked at the trucker and wondered to himself if this was a good idea. After coming all this way, being so close to home the thought of dying in a horrific crash because this old man has a heart attack was a little unsettling.

The old man walked up to Hans and stuck out his hand to shake Hans's and said, "Hi son, I am Gordon, what's your name?"

"My name is Hans, sir. Thank you for giving me a lift, I greatly appreciate it," Hans said to Gordon.

"No problem, son, it will be nice having someone to talk to on the drive," Gordon said. "The truck should be loaded in about ten more minutes then we can be on our way. Come over here and sit with us and have some coffee."

"Thank you, sir," Hans replied and sat down with the truckers to wait for the truck to be loaded.

Once the truck was loaded Hans and Gordon crawled into the cab of the truck to get underway. Hans looked at Gordon sitting in the driver's seat and a look of worry came over his face. Hans was correct in his earlier assumption, Gordon could barely see over the steering wheel. Gordon saw the look on Hans's face and knew exactly what he was thinking. "Don't worry, son, I have been driving for thirty-five years and I haven't lost a load yet," Gordon said to Hans. He gave Hans a little wink and revved the engine three times and popped the clutch. The truck jerked forward with terrific force and Hans was shoved back in his seat. He quickly grabbed the handle to the door with his right hand and the seat with his left. His eyes grew large and there was an undeniable look of fear in his face. Gordon looked at Hans and snickered. "I got you boy, got you good."

"Oh lord," Hans thought to himself. "I am with an elderly version of Sven and he is driving, I am definitely going to die."

"Well, son, we have got two hours to kill until we reach Osby, let's do a little talking," Gordon said. "Is Osby home?"

"Yes, sir," Hans replied. "I have lived there all my life."

"You got a girl back home?" Gordon asked.

"Yes, sir, and I will marry her as soon as I get home," Hans replied.

"That's wonderful, son, is she a good woman?" Gordon asked.

"She is the best woman I have ever known. She is kind and gentle and she would go out of her way to help anyone in need. I feel like I am the luckiest man in the world to have her," Hans said.

"She really must be something special, your face lights up when you talk about her. Just like mine did when I fell in love with my Helga, she was a wonderful woman," Gordon said. "There is nothing like the love of a good women, they will forever change your life for the better, whether you like it or not," Gordon said with a big smile.

"You must have been a lucky man too," Hans said.

"Yes, I was," Gordon replied. "She was an angel, definitely too good for the likes of me. Maybe that's why the good lord took her from me," Gordon said sadly.

"I am so sorry, Gordon," Hans said. "I don't know if I could go on if I lost Carina."

"You go on," Gordon said to Hans. "It's just a lonely and painful existence sometimes."

Hans and Gordon drove the rest of the way to Osby pretty much in silence, both were reflecting on the women they love. Hans forever grateful for the woman he loves and Gordon in sorrow for the love he had lost. They reached Osby late in the afternoon. Gordon stopped the truck for Hans to get out.

"Thank you for the lift, Gordon, it was very nice to meet you. Be careful out there and I wish you all the best to you, sir."

"Good luck, son," Gordon replied. "Remember, treat her right you never know how long you will have her."

"I will, sir," Hans smiled at Gordon, shook his hand in gratitude and got out of the truck.

Hans watched the truck pull away and drive out of sight. He thought of Gordon and Helga and how Gordon painfully mourns for her. Hans said a short prayer in his head in hope that he would never have to feel the anguish Gordon has to suffer with the rest of the days of his life. Hans began to walk to his mother's house. It felt so good to be home and to see old familiar sites. He walked up the hill on the old dirt road and his mother's house came into sight. To Hans's surprise Carina was there, sweeping off the front porch.

Hans had caught Carina's attention out of the corner of her eye. Carina looked up to get a view of what she thought she had seen. She could not believe her eyes, it was Hans. Tears of joy immediately began to flow from her eyes and she shook from excitement and disbelief from what she was seeing from head to toe. Carina dropped the broom and ran to Hans. She jumped on Hans wrapping her legs around his waist and grasping his head in her hands. The force of Carina's momentum caused Hans to fall to the ground. She was straddled on top of Hans and began to kiss his whole face over and over. In her excitement she didn't realize Hans was reeling in pain from the wound he had received at the front. Carina pushed herself up and away from Hans's face. "Oh Hans, I have waited so long for you," Carina said. Carina looked Hans in the face and could tell he was in extreme pain. "What is wrong, Hans, are you hurt?" Carina asked.

"It is just a small souvenir from the Caucuses," Hans told Carina.

"Come inside and let me take care of you," Carina said to Hans. Carina grabbed Hans by the hand and pulled him into the house. Carina escorted Hans by the hand to the dining room table. Carina helped Hans to take off his shirt so that she could see his wound and gently pushed Hans down in the chair. She knelt down then pulled back on the bandage covering Hans's wound. Carina looked at the wound and a worried look came over her face. "Is it bad?" She asked.

"No, it's much better. Don't you worry, I will be fine, it's healing up nicely," Hans replied.

"No, Hans, the front. Is it just horrible? Please don't lie," Carina asked sincerely.

"I won't lie to you, sweetheart, it's bad but it is something we must do. If we don't, one day Russia will be at our boarder. We must cut the head off before it strikes," Hans said with conviction.

"Do you have to go back?" Carina asked.

"Not for now, but don't think of that right now. We have more important things to think about, like our wedding," Hans said. Then he bent down and kissed Carina on the forehead. Carina immediately smiled and you could see the look of joy in her face thinking of her day to be wed.

CHAPTER TEN

"IT'S GOING TO BE the most beautiful wedding ever," Carina proclaimed. "Are you hungry, Hans?" Carina asked.

"I am starving," Hans replied. "I am craving your Raggmunk. I haven't had that since I left home." Raggmunk is the name for a Swedish potato pancake. The pancakes are fried in butter and served with fried pork.

"I will fix some for you," Carina said smiling at Hans.

"Thank you, sweetheart, will you show me where momma is buried tomorrow?" Hans asked.

"Of course I will, darling, I will pick some fresh flowers for her in the morning then we can go," Carina said. "We also need to go by my parents' house. They are dying to see you as well. Oh my god, Hans, I am so sorry. I didn't mean it that way. What the hell is wrong with me?"

"It's okay, sweetheart, I know what you meant. I can't wait to see them either," Hans said with a smile.

After Hans and Carina ate, he watched her as she scurried around the house gathering items and placed them in front of the fireplace. She had gathered a blanket, wine, cheese, and two candles. As Carina walked about Hans was almost entranced with her. When she walked it was as if she was gliding across the floor. Her neck was dainty and delicate and her feet were tiny. Carina had big brown eyes and the smile of a little girl. Hans wondered how he ever got so lucky to get a girl like Carina and at the same time wondered what was wrong with her for liking a guy like him. Whatever it was, Hans was glad for it, he couldn't imagine being with anyone else.

Carina spread out the blanket, started a fire, and opened the wine. "Come sit with me, Hans," she said patting the blanket. Hans joined Carina in front of the fire. Carina poured them both a glass of wine and handed one of the glasses to Hans. "Cheers, honey, welcome home." Carina toasted.

"Thank you, Carina, it is so good to finally be here. It feels like I have been away so long," Hans said.

"You have, you jerk. I want you home to stay," Carina said with a pout.

"I know you do, Carina. This war won't last very long and then soon I will be home for good, I promise," Hans tried to say as convincingly as possible. He knew that the Russians were putting up a pretty good fight and the way they seemed to multiply their numbers with endless reserves of men, tanks, and supplies, they might be in store for a very long war. Carina leaped at Hans wrapping her arms around his neck throwing her full weight on Hans's shoulders. Hans once again fell to the ground under the weight of Carina's passionate attack. Hans loudly moans out in pain as his body hits the floor.

"Oh my god! I am so sorry, Hans, are you okay?" Carina asked tense and concerned.

"I see nothing has changed," Hans grumbled. Carina was perfect in every way to Hans but for one dangerous flaw. She was as clumsy as a drunken sailor. "I am beginning to wonder if it might be safer for me back at the front," Hans teasingly says to Carina.

"No one back there can take care of you like I can," Carina said seductively and kissed Hans slow and gently on his lips. "I love you, Hans," Carina said.

"I love you too, Carina," Hans replied.

Carina leaned over Hans and passionately kissed him. Their bodies were pressed together but they both tried to get even closer to one another. They held each other in their arms gently petting each other. Hans grasps Carina's breast and gently squeezes. Carina quietly moans and rolls her head back. Feeling Hans touching her made her feel wonderful and she desperately wanted more but she couldn't.

"No, Hans, we can't," Carina said reluctantly.

"Why?" Hans asked.

"I want my first time to be special. I want to be your bride. I hope you can understand, Hans, it's important to me."

"It's okay, Carina, I can wait. I have waited all these years I think I can handle a few more days," Hans said.

"Thank you. After we get married I am going to make you happy over and over again for the rest of your life," Carina said like a naughty girl. Hans knew that Carina was a woman of her word and Hans was good with that.

The next morning Hans awoke to sausage and eggs being served to him in bed. "Good morning, sunshine, rise and shine," Carina said with a big smile.

"Wow, what's all this?" Hans asked rubbing the sleep out of his eyes.

"It's a thank you," Carina said.

"For what?" Hans asked.

"For loving me," Carina replied and danced out of the room.

"I could really get used to this," Hans said to himself then dove into his food.

One of the things Hans loved about Carina is that she was a good cook, as good as his mother and no one was as good as Momma. It was so nice being home with all the creature comforts it provides and the food, so much better than the rancid meat and crackers they get at the front. That stuff is only good enough for dogs and Sven, Hans had a more sensitive pallet. Hans finished breakfast, got dressed, and went downstairs to meet Carina.

Carina had already picked a beautiful bouquet of wildflowers to bring to his mother's grave. "Aren't they lovely, Hans, I just love this time of year," Carina sighed.

"They are very nice, Carina, thank you," Hans said. "Are you ready to go?"

"I'm ready," Carina said.

"Okay, let's go," Hans replied.

Walking to the cemetery, Carina strikes a conversation with Hans. "Hans, what does it all mean? Why are we here, what is this all for? What is the purpose of our lives?" Carina asked.

"I think we are all put here to help each other. I think we are here to be as kind and nurturing to one another as we can," Hans said.

"Hans, you're a soldier and you kill your fellow man, isn't that cruel and unkind?" Carina asked.

"Which is more cruel, Carina, killing to keep millions from becoming enslaved or doing nothing and letting millions become enslaved?" Hans asked her.

"I see your point," Carina said. "It does seem to be the lesser of two evils. This is why I can take pride in what I do. I am a soldier and a good one. I can make a difference and defend those who cannot defend themselves. I am helping keep communism from destroying our society. Not to mention keeping innocent men, women, and children from being raped, tortured, and murdered by those damn communists," Hans said with devout conviction.

They continue on their walk in relative silence reflecting upon the war. Hans is contemplating his return to the war and Carina, the desire for Hans to return from the war forever.

The following morning, Hans and Carina were just finishing up with breakfast when a knock came to the door. "I wonder who that could be this early in the morning," Carina said. She walked to the door and opened it. There stood two of Hans's friends and four of Carina's friends. They were there to kidnap them both for a stag do.

In Sweden they don't have the traditional western custom of a bachelor's party consisting of drunken debauchery and strippers. Traditionally it is customary for the soon to be bride and groom to be kidnapped by their friends for one or two days. The stag dos (or bachelor parties) or hen party (bachelorette bash) consists of fun activities the group of them can do together as if it was their last chance to play together as free men or women. Normally the other partner knows that this will happen and will lie to make sure that they are in the right place at the right time.

Sometimes friends will plan the bachelor and bachelorette festivities to fall on the same day so they both have to try and fool each other. Pulling pranks on the guests of honor is also a big part of the tradition. Hans and Carina's friends grab them by the arms and drag them out of the house to two waiting cars. The men pile in one car and the women in the other. As they drive away the sound of the men singing a silly sea Chianti and the women giggling like a group of school girls slowly fades away.

Hans has known Elise and Erik since childhood and they were the two orneriest guys he had ever met. Elise and Erik took Hans to Kariskrona a port town on the coast. Erick had a friend that owned a large boat and owed him a favor. Hans had always wanted to captain a ship but had never got the opportunity so Erick set it up so that they could help fulfill on of Hans's dreams. There was only one condition—Hans had to wear a fake beard that Erik and Elise had made for him.

"No, I don't think I am going to wear that silly beard," Hans said to Erik. "It looks ridiculous."

"You have to, Hans, that's the rule," Erik said. "Besides, all boat captains have beards."

"Okay," Hans said reluctantly and put the beard on. Hans spent the day at the helm of his ship. It was fun to live out one of your dreams and Hans was very grateful to his friends for their wonderful gift.

After spending the day on the water they decided to go to have a steam bath, another traditional Swedish activity. The three men undressed and got into the bath. Hans couldn't help but notice that the private areas of Elise and Erick were both shaven. "I don't mean to pry but I have to ask, why are you both shaven down there?" Hans asked. Elise and Erick both looked at each other and smiled mischievously then Erik turned to Hans and said. "Where do you think we got the hair for the beard from?"

"You sick bastards!" Hans says with a hint of disbelief while his friends laugh hysterically at him. "Are you saying I spent the whole day wearing your pubic hair on my face?" Hans asked.

"Yes, yes, you did," Erik says while chuckling.

"You assholes!" Hans said. "Well, you got me. You dumbasses got me good."

Where hen dos and stag parties differ is in the treatment of the bride and groom from their friends. The object of a stag party is to humiliate and poke fun at the groom as much as possible. Hen dos, on the other hand, are about solidifying relationships in an evening where inhibitions can be set free under the protection of the group. Carina and her friends had reservations at hotel Concordia in Malmo. They got settled in their rooms and were preparing for an evening out on the town. Carina was in her room freshening up from the trip when a knock came on the door of her room. She opened the door and there stood her friend Elsa holding up a bottle of vodka with a mischievous smile on her face from ear to ear.

Elsa was the bad girl of the group, she was one of those girls that other girls seem to hate and envy at the same time. It was as if her life was one big party and the party was only interrupted by romantic interludes with new men. "Want to have a good time, sailor?" Elsa asked.

Carina smiled at Elsa. "Get in here, silly," Carina said. Elsa walks in and Carina shuts the door behind her.

"Where are you girls taking me tonight?" Carina curiously asked.

"That is a secret, my dear," Elsa replies. "Come on, Elsa, tell me, I am dying to know," Carina pleads. "Come have a drink of this, it will calm you down. Besides, it's good for your soul," Elsa said.

"I'm sure it is," Carina replied and took a drink of the vodka.

After Carina had swallowed a mouthful of vodka she began to choke and gasp. "How the hell do you drink that stuff like that, it's terrible!" Carina said gasping.

"It is just like sex, it gets more enjoyable the more times you do it," Elsa said with a smile. Carina and Elsa continued to take shots of vodka over the afternoon. Carina wasn't quite the drinker Elsa was. Carina had lived a little more reserved life.

CHAPTER ELEVEN

BY THE TIME IT had come to get together with the other girls for the evening's events Carina was very drunk. "I think I am going to be sick," Carina said with a slur and began to lightly heave. Elsa quickly grabbed the wash basin off of the dresser and put it under Carina's face.

"I guess the party has begun," Elsa said sarcastically. A knock came from the door and Elsa walked to the door and opened it. It was the rest of the girls that came to get Carina for the evening.

They were all smiles, excitedly jumping up and down in anticipation of the evening. Carina struggles to get to her feet, stumbles over to the bed and collapses. "The whole room is spinning," Carina mumbles. The smiles on the girls' faces fall to the floor. They all look at Elsa expecting an explanation on how Carina could possibly get in that condition. The girls immediately knew Elsa had something to do with it.

"Carina's not feeling well, she is not going to make it tonight but she wants us to go have a good time for her," Elsa said. The girls looked at Carina lying on the bed and a look of concern and sympathy came over their faces. "Come on, girls, we have Malmo waiting for us," Elsa said as she pushed the girls out of the doorway into the hall closing the door behind her. The girls begin to walk down the hall. "I will meet you in the lobby, I have to go back to the room I forgot my pocketbook!" Elsa shouted running back to Carina's room.

Elsa entered Carina's room, spotted her handbag on the dresser and walked over to retrieve it. She turned to leave but stopped and sat on the edge of Carina's bed. Elsa brushed back some hair off Carinas sleeping face. "Even knowing how crappy you're going to feel in the morning, I still wish I were you," Elsa said, then bent down and kissed Carina on the forehead. She stood up and walked out the door closing it behind her. As she closed the door she stopped and looked at Carina lying on the bed. Elsa smiled, shook her head, and lightly chuckled then slowly closed the door.

The wedding day had finally arrived. Vows were to be said on the dock on a beautiful lake at Carina's parents' home. The view overlooking the lake was almost breathtaking. Carina had been planning her wedding there since she was a young girl and now her dream was to finally coming to pass. There were cousins and aunts and uncles and friends of both Hans and Carina. It was everyone she had known and even several that she didn't. It was a beautiful day and it seemed as if nothing could go wrong.

Unlike the west, traditionally in Sweden the father of the bride does not walk her down the aisle. The bride meets the groom and as a couple walk hand in hand down the aisle to stand before the priest to take their vows. Hans meets Carina at the bridge to the dock to walk her to where the priest, the best man, and the maid of honor await their arrival. Hans takes Carina's hand in to his and says to her, "I love you, Carina."

"I love you too, Hans," Carina replies.

Hans and Carina proceed to walk down the length of the dock. Just as Hans and Carina reach the end of the dock where the priest is waiting, Carina's heel of her shoe gets caught between two boards on the dock tripping her. Carina falls into the priest and both he and Carina fall into the cold waters of the lake. All the guests gasp in unison then the gasps convert into hardy laughter as Hans, the best man, and maid of honor try to fish Carina and the priest out of the water.

Hans leans over the edge of the dock and stretches out his hand in an effort to grab Carina. "Carina, grab my hand," Hans says to Carina trying desperately not to laugh. Carina grabs Hans's hand and he pulls her out of the water. Carina soaking wet, shaking from the cold and crying says, "It's ruined, Hans, it's all ruined."

"No, it's not," Hans replied with a reassuring smile. "It's just memorable now." Carina was crying, her eye makeup smeared on her face and Hans looking at her smiling in loving admiration at the woman he could not live without. They then continued with their vows to one another transforming their two lives into one.

The young couple's days together quickly one by one drifted by. Hans's wound was almost healed and it was near time to return to Berlin to receive his orders to return to his unit. Hans would soon have to say goodbye and leave his perfect life in exchange for hell at the front. Hans had read in the paper that the Russians were overwhelming the Germans and that the Germans were now in retreat. Things were not going as Hitler had planned. Hitler had not anticipated the resolve of the Russians and their endless supply of men and material.

Germany's supply lines were stretched thin and they could not keep up with the demand of the supplies needed to support any strategic advancement or even sufficient supplies for withdraw due to the great distances they had to maneuver. Roads in Russia, if there were any, were muddy bogs at best and in the winter temperature would plummet below freezing. Tanks, trucks, and equipment would freeze in the mud sealing them to the ground like cement.

The German Army had not been supplied for winter fighting, they had no winter coats only summer uniforms. Some days the temperature would be below thirty degrees. Men were freezing and starving to death. Over one hundred thousand Germans surrendered to the Russians knowing they would either be shot or sent to a Russian concentration camp. Just to keep from starvation or becoming another soldier's meal. Times were desperate, the food was gone. They were unable to be supplied. They had eaten all of their horses and it was rumored that some soldiers were doing the unthinkable in an effort to keep themselves alive.

Carina and her parents drove Hans to Trelleborg to see him off so he could catch the ferry back to Germany. Standing at the pear Carina sees the ferry pull in to the dock for boarding. Carina starts to cry and puts her arms around Hans. "Don't go, Hans, stay here with me," Carina pleads. "You don't owe the Germans anything. It's their war not ours." Hans smiles as if to reassure Carina that everything will be fine. Hans Hugs Carina and kisses her passionately.

"I took an oath to fight and you know I am a man of my word. Sweetheart, if a man doesn't stand by his word he is not much of a man," Hans explained.

"I know you are, Hans, I just want you home where you belong, not putting your life in danger for some insane ideology. Hitler is mad and Germany is going to lose the war. Germany is fighting the Russians, the French, the English and now the Americans. There is no way Hitler can win this war," Carina said tearfully.

"Don't worry so much," Hans said. "The French conquered, the Americans are too busy with the Japanese and even if the Americans did try to cross the channel with the British they would never be successful in invading Europe. The Atlantic wall defenses are impenetrable. This means all we really have to concern ourselves with is the Russians and they will be defeated once the Germans regroup and are resupplied.

Don't worry your pretty little head, everything will be just fine and I will be right back home before you know it," Hans said with conviction. The time came For Hans to say goodbye and aboard the ferry to Germany. Carina's father extends his hand to Hans to shake his. "Good luck, Hans, be careful and keep your head down, I have grown accustomed to that face. Besides, you're the only son I have. I need you around to take care of the farm when I get old."

"Yes, sir, I will," Hans replied with a smile.

Hans leaned over to get close to Carina's ear and murmured, "Who could resist that," sarcastically.

Carina's mother hugged Hans and said, "Do be careful, Hans, we all love you very much."

"Yes, Mamma," Hans replied with a loving smile. A shout from the ferry notifying everyone that it was their last opportunity to board and that the ferry was ready to leave. Hans quickly gave Carina a quick kiss on the lips and said, "I love you and I will write as soon as I get to my duty station."

Hans rushed down the pier to board the ferry waiving to Carina as he ran. Carina and her parents shouted "Goodbye! Be careful, we all love you!" as Hans boarded. The ship began to sail away, Hans stayed at the stern of the ship looking back at Carina until she was out of site. Hans's heart felt very heavy and he wondered to himself if it would be the last time he sees his Carina. Hans knew there was still a lot of war left to fight and the odds for survival were not in his favor.

Hans had made it to Berlin but Berlin was not the same city he had seen before. Blocks and blocks of destroyed and burnt out buildings. It was if it were just the skeleton of the city he once knew. As Hans walked through the rubble filled streets he could see women and children's bodies thrown about, mangled and burnt. Children so disfigured they were unrecognizable even to a mother.

The Americans had been bombing the city in the daylight hours and the British at night, killing thousands of civilians with each attack turning the city into a nightmarish burning hell. There was no water, no sewer, very little food, and death all around them but the Berliners refused to give up on their Fuhrer. They all believed that Hitler had a master plan and some secret weapon under development that would save Germany then Hitler would lead them on to victory.

"What was this spell that Hitler had over the Germans" Hans pondered as he made his way through the burned out streets of Berlin. Anyone with any sense can see that things are not going well for Germany and Hitler was leading them down a path of total destruction. The war had now reached a turning point. It was no longer a war to stop communism, it was now a war of survival and Hans could plainly see that now.

Hans arrived at the headquarters of the Reich Main Security Office, SD, Gestapo and the SS building to receive his assignment orders. Hans walked inside the building. It was very bright and sunny outside and the inside of the building was dark and Hans could hardly see until his eyes adjusted to the darkness. Before Hans's eyes could adjust he ran into someone standing in the entryway knocking them to the ground. "You idiot!" said the man knocked to the ground. "Look where you're going."

"I am so sorry," Hans said as he grabbed the arm of the man on the floor to help him up. "My eyes hadn't adjusted to the light and I couldn't see you."

"Ah, Swede, I can tell by the accent," said the man. Hans's eyesight adjusted to the light and he looked into the man's face.

81

Hans couldn't believe his eyes it was *Reichsfuhrer* (general of the SS) Heinrich Himmler. Hans had seen the man in propaganda films but never thought he would meet him in person.

"I haven't been to Sweden in years but when I was there I loved it, great memories. What's your name, son?" Himmler asked.

"Hans Gruber, sir," Hans replied.

"What's your business here, Hans?" Himmler asked.

"I am here to get my orders to return to my unit. I was wounded and sent on leave so I went home and married the most wonderful woman in the world," Hans said almost as if he were boasting.

"What's your unit, soldier?" Himmler asked.

"I'm a Wiking, sir, Fifth SS," Hans replied. "Great unit, Wiking, I have always had good reports on you boys," Himmler said. "Wait here and I will send someone to help you. Good hunting, soldier, Heil Hitler!" Himmler said with a stern look on his face. Hans snapped his heels together and returned the Nazi salute. "Heil Hitler!" Hans replied to his surprise, almost instinctively as Himmler walks away. Hans grins as a thought quickly enters his mind watching Himmler walk away. "Strange, he looks taller in the news reels."

CHAPTER TWELVE

HANS RECEIVES HIS ORDERS and he was to report back to the Fifth SS Wiking division. In the summer of 1943 the Fifth SS Panzer Division and Twenty third Panzer Division, formed the reserve force for Operation Citadel. Immediately following the German defeat in the Battle of Kursk, the Red Army launched counteroffensives, known as Operations Kutuzov and Rumyantsev. Wiking, together with SS Division Das Reich and SS Division Totenkopf, were assigned to the Mius-Bogodukhov sector.

The Soviets overran Kharkov on the twenty third of August and began advancing towards the Dnieper River. The Russians were smashing through the German lines like a steamroller and it was as if nothing could stop them. The Dnieper became a natural barrier the Russians would have to navigate while continuously under fire from the German Army. It would not be an easy undertaking for the Russians to cross that river and break through the German lines but that did not matter.

Russia would gladly sacrifice ten men to kill one German if that's what it took and the Russians had an endless supply of manpower to back it up. They were coming and the German soldiers began to see the writing on the wall. Germany was going to lose the war. Germany could not beat the Soviets consistently in battle, they could not hold them to a stalemate, so they could only try and delay the inevitable as long as they possibly can.

When Hans arrived at the Dnieper he did not return to the proud and victorious Waffen-SS he had left when he was wounded. Moral was bad, the men were constantly dirty and sleep deprived. There was little food, ammunition was low. There was very little air support if any at all. The number of tanks had been depleted by sixty percent and the infantry by forty percent. Any replacements brought to the front became younger and younger. They looked as if they were boys taken from the Hitler youth.

Hans found Wiking headquarters and reported for duty. Hans was assigned duty in the first platoon and was then pointed in the direction where first platoon had dug in. Hans thought how he is going to miss his bed at home. "It looks like it's sleeping in foxholes from now on," Hans said to himself. "What the hell was I thinking?" Hans said in disbelief at what he had given up to be here. He shook his head and snickered to himself then began to walk toward his new platoon.

As Hans passed an area the unit had designated as a location for a latrine, he heard a familiar voice. "Hans, is that you?" Hans turned to look and to his great delight it was Sven. Sven was walking toward Hans buttoning up his trousers with a huge smile on his face. "Sven," Hans said. "You're still alive."

"I keep telling you, Hans, I'm too pretty to die," Sven replied. Hans and Sven gave each other a huge bear hug. It was as if being reunited with a long lost brother. They pulled away from the hug and looked at each other in the face. They could both see that the other was teary-eyed with joy. The big strong warriors hugged each other once again patting one another on the back. "Welcome home, Hans, how's the wound?" Sven asked.

"Much better now, almost like new," Hans replied.

"How is everyone back home, anything interesting going on back home?" Sven asked.

"I married Carina," Hans said.

"You're a lucky man, Hans, Carina is a good woman. There are not many finer than her," Sven said.

"It was a beautiful wedding, the one Carina always wanted out on the lake at her parents' house," Hans said.

"That sounds nice," Sven replied.

"Want to hear something funny?" Hans asked Sven. Sven smiles and nods yes. "Carina and I were walking down the aisle on the dock when Carina tripped, stumbled in to the priest knocking them both into the lake. Carina looked so cute looking up at me crying and soaking wet from head to toe, she reminded me of a helpless little girl."

"I see Carina hasn't changed," Sven said laughingly. "Carina's no ballerina," Sven said as he had said a hundred times teasing Carina when they were children.

"Carina was humiliated and mad as hell until I told her that it will be the fondest thing we think of about our wedding for the rest of our lives, you have made a wonderful memory."

Sven smiled and said. "It doesn't get better than that, I can't think of something better to remember. Well, here we are buddy, home sweet home," Sven said jokingly. Before them on the ground, lay a muddy eight by three foot hole with a young man about seventeen years old standing in it. "Okay, Hans, which side of the bed would you like to sleep on?" Sven said with just a touch of sarcasm.

"I will take the left side," Hans said. "So, who is your young friend?"

"This is young William or as I like to call him, Little Willy," Sven replied. "He just transferred in from training yesterday, it's his first day of work so don't expect too much."

"That's okay, kid, we were all green once. Stick by us and you will be just fine and don't try to be a hero you will just end up dead like the other heros," Hans says in a fatherly tone then gently pats William on the shoulder in reassurance. "Sven, you take the first watch, I will take the second, and sir William will take the third," Hans said with authority.

"You sure have gotten bossy since you left," Sven said jokingly.

"That's odd, Carina has been bossy since we got married too. There must be something in the air," Hans said with a smile.

"All right I am going to try and get some sleep," Hans said as he crouched down in the foxhole.

"Sweet dreams, princess," Sven said in a loud whisper.

"Ah. That's what I like about you, Sven." Hans yawns and stretches out his arms. "You are always so considerate of others," Hans mumbles as he quickly drifts off to sleep.

Sven wakes Hans for his shift in the watch kicking Hans's leg. Hans quickly awakens and stands up for a lookout of the foxhole next to Sven. Hans could clearly hear all the noise the Russians were making across the river. The sound of trucks, tanks, and men talking and moving about with no effort to move in secrecy as if they were wanting the Germans to know they were massing several armies for an attack. It was a type of psychological warfare. "They have been doing this for hours," Sven said to Hans. They must be planning for something big. Keep your eyes open, Hans, they are sneaky bastards."

"I will, my friend, get some rest," Hans replied. The Russians continues to make noise as if maneuvering all through Hans's watch. Hans woke William for his shift at watch. He briefed William on what had been going on during the night. "All that noises are probably to distract us from something else that's going on. Keep your eyes open and if you hear anything, don't shout out. Kick me in the leg. We want to make as little noise as possible so we can surprise them when they attack. You okay, kid?" Hans asked William.

"Sure," William said as Hans was crouching back down in the foxhole in an attempt to get a couple more hours of sleep. "Hey," William said. "Thanks for being so nice to me. You're the only one since I got here."

"Just keep you head down and eyes open, and wake me in the morning," Hans said.

Hans struggled to sleep the rest of the night. He had a feeling all hell was going to break loose in the morning but it wasn't the fear of the enemy that kept Hans awake, it was the fear of never to be able to see Carina again. He kept thinking about all the days he has spent with Carina and the things they have done together while drifting in and out of sleep. Thirty minutes after daybreak William woke Hans and Sven, then briefed them of the activities of the enemy on his watch.

Sven was still crouched down in the foxhole slowly woke. William was looking out of the foxhole trying to keep track of enemy movement. "Get up you lazy turd," Hans said to Sven as he was bending over to slap Sven on the helmet. As Hans's hand hit the top of Sven's helmet there was a large explosion a feet away from their foxhole. The Russians have started their attack with an artillery barrage. The explosion blows off young William's head but his body stayed in the same standing position and did not fall to the ground. Hans and Sven look at each other in disbelief. "Looks like it's time to earn our pay," Sven said with a smile and the boys prepared themselves for a Soviet assault.

The Russian artillery barrage lasted about two hours then suddenly ended. Thousands of high explosive rounds were hurtled into German lines surprisingly only killing a few men. Hans and Sven could hear the Russians yelling their battle cry as they began their ground assault. They could see the Russian soldiers running down the other bank of the river dragging with them small boats to cross the river in. The enemy began to cross the river and the German artillery and mortars began to open fire and the shells began to rain down on the Russians.

The artillery shells were landing on the other river bank creating huge craters throwing dirt and bodied high into the air killing many Russians as they tried to make it down to the river. As the Russians began to cross the river mortar shells were fired into the river in an effort to kill as many as possible before they reached the German held side of the river. Rarely did a mortar land directly on a boat but they would land close enough to the boats to be effective.

The mortars would explode under water and the power of the explosion would force water high in the air. If the boats were close enough to the geyser like explosions the pressure of the water from under the boat was enough to capsize the small boats throwing the soldiers inside them into the dark muddy water. The Russian soldiers would desperately struggle and try to stay afloat calling out for help as they flayed about in the water, but the weight of their weapons and ammunition they carried weighed them down and they soon succumbed to death's solid grasp.

Hans and Sven were watching the chaos of the battle from their foxhole. "It's just amazing," Sven said to Hans.

"What are you talking about?" Hans asked.

"The huge explosions, the noise, and the movement of hundreds of men, it's almost beautiful," Sven said with a subtle sense of glee.

"You are a very strange man, Sven, Mamma told me to stay away from you but of course I didn't listen. Mamma was a very wise woman, I should have listened," Hans said teasingly. Hans and Sven smiled at each other then their attention turned back to the battle.

The Russians began to assemble on the bank of the German held side of the river preparing for an assault up the hill toward the positions held by Hans and the rest of the Wiking division. "You ready for this, Sven, it looks like it's going to get a little hairy," Hans said concerned about the situation they were in.

Sven replies as if he were indestructible. "You just worry about yourself, I keep telling you . . ."

Hans interrupts Sven in mid-sentence. "I know, I know you're too pretty to die. You just keep your head down dumbass," Hans said authoritatively. Sven give Hans a wink and a smile and looks back down at the assembling Russians.

CHAPTER THIRTEEN

A WHISTLE BLEW AND the Russians began their assault up the hill towards Hans and Sven's position. They waited until the Russian soldiers became close enough to make sure they could get a kill with each shot fired. Ammunition was low and the Germans had to make every round count. Halfway up the bank of the river the Russians came within range of Hans and Sven and they began to fire into the oncoming onslaught.

Russian soldier after soldier fell, slaughtered by the overwhelming firepower of the German defense, but the Russian soldiers kept coming and coming in an endless supply of men. Hans and Sven were soon out of ammunition and the situation became desperate. "I'm out of ammo!" Sven shouted.

"I am too!" Hans replied. "Fix bayonets, let's go!" Hans ordered.

Hans crawled out of the foxhole and made a stance in preparation of the hand to hand combat that was inevitably going to come. Sven joined Hans at his side just as two Russian soldiers begin to attack them. Hans thrusts his bayonet at the Russian but the soldier parries Hans's rifle and knocks it out of his hands. The Russian attempts to butt Hans in the face with his rifle but Hans quickly grabs the rifle and falls to the ground letting his weight pull the Russian to the ground as well.

Hans and the Russian began to wrestle on the ground then they both jumped to their feet. The Russian reached for his rifle and as he did Hans pulled his SS dagger out of its sheath on his belt. Hans plunges the dagger deep in the side of the neck of the Russian soldier. Hans's dagger severed the main artery in the Russian's neck and blood shoots from his neck and into Sven's face, momentarily blinding him.

The Russian soldier then goes limp and falls to the ground. Sven, temporarily blinded could not see the other Russian soldier attacking him. The Russian thrusts his bayonet at Sven and the blade goes through the back of Sven's arm completely threw the arm halfway between the elbow and shoulder. Sven grabs his arm and falls to the ground in pain. Hans quickly retrieves his rifle from the ground and attempts to kill the Russian before he kills Sven.

Hans raises his rifle into position in an attempt to bayonet the remaining soldier, but as he did a stray round fired from some unknown direction hits Hans's rifle ripping it in half but not injuring Hans. The rifle had just saved Hans's life but was now useless. Both Hans and the Russian soldier stop and look at each other in dis belief of what had just happened. The reality of the situation quickly reentered Hans's head. He knew that he was in real trouble, he now had no weapon.

As the Russian was still looking at Hans in amazement at what had just taken place, Hans pulls off his helmet and hits the Russian soldier in the face as hard as he could with his helmet. The Russian falls to the ground and Hans jumps on top of him and repeatedly hits the Russian in his face with his helmet until he was killed. Hans didn't mind killing the Russians but he was not a morbid man. It bothered Hans that he had to kill that young soldier so brutally.

A quick, clean kill was much more humane. Hans suddenly noticed that it had got quiet, there was no more weapons being fired. They must have held off the Russian advance one more time. Hans escorted Sven back to the medical station setup for the wounded and a nurse patched him up. "I am sorry we don't have anything to help with the pain, all we have is a little cognac to offer," the nurse said sympathetically.

"I may need a lot, nurse, I am in some very bad pain," Sven said with a puppy face.

"Oh, no, you don't." Hans said. "I am not going to stay in a foxhole with you drunk all night. He's fine, nurse. Let's go, little girl," Hans said as he pulled Sven off of the medical stretcher and they began walking back to their foxhole.

As the boys were walking they notice quite a commotion going on ahead of them. There were SS men pouring fuel on the outside of a church. Hans noticed a couple of guys from the Wiking division were standing on the road watching them. Hans and Sven walked up to one of the men and asked "What's going on?" The soldier told Hans that the men were from the Einsatzgruppen and that they were about to burn the church.

The Einsatzgruppen were mobile killing units. Squads composed primarily of German SS. They were under the command of the *Sicherheitspolizei* (The German Security Police) and the *Sicherheitsdienst* (The Security Service). The Einsatzgruppen had among their tasks the murder of any of those deemed to be racial or political enemies of the Third Reich found behind German lines in the occupied areas of the Soviet Union.

Jews, communists, homosexuals and the mentally ill were just a few of those they were assigned to exterminate. Hans walked over to one of the Einsatzgruppen men and asks, "Why are you burning down this church?"

"Because there are two hundred Jews in it silly, Jews free in '43," the soldier said to Hans with a big grin on his face. Hans couldn't believe what he had just heard and looked at Sven in disbelief. The Einsatzgruppen took a flame thrower around the building lighting the church on fire from all four sides. Inside the church was quiet at first but as the smoke and flames began to fill the building screams could be heard from the inside. A few women and children screaming at first but then the cries began to increase. Now men, women, and children could be heard frantically screaming in horror as they were slowly burned alive. The screams peaked in a chorus of misery then slowly dissipated into a sedative silence. There was the sickening sweet smell of burning flesh all through the air and the only sound was the crackling of the fire.

The Einsatzgruppen soldiers stood there with a look of pride in their faces as they watched the church burn. Proud of the work they have done for the betterment of the Father Land and of the glorious Third Reich. Hans and Sven walk back to their foxhole, along the way Hans said, "Killing your enemy is one thing but murdering civilian women and children like that is another, how could someone do that?"

"I have heard several stories like that since you have been away," Sven said remorsefully. "Hitler said that he wanted a Jew-free Europe and the fanatical Nazis are killing every Jew they find. I couldn't believe it at first either, but now that I have seen it in person I find it a bit disconcerting. Is that what we are fighting for?" Sven asks.

"Wow," Hans said. "When did you become empathetic, that's not the Sven I have always known."

"People change, Hans, try to keep up," Sven said then jumped down into the foxhole. Hans rolls his eyes at Sven's ridiculous remark and jumps down into the foxhole with him.

A young SS soldier runs up to Hans's foxhole with supply cans of ammunition for them.

"Did you guys hear what happed to the Walloons?" the soldier asks. The Walloons are a unit in the Waffen-SS consisting of Belgian volunteers.

"No, what happened?" Hans asked.

"The Walloons had a bunch of Russian volunteers fighting alongside them against the communists. Last night the Russian volunteers slit the throats of the Walloon sentries and defected to the communists. They have our battle plans, the locations of our gun emplacements and where every soldier on the front line is located. Expect an attack and to be overrun at any moment. Be ready to get the hell out of here if you can. Good luck guys," the young soldier said then he ran to get more ammunition for the next foxhole in the line. Another young SS soldier runs up to Hans's foxhole. "Are either of you Gruber?" the soldier asked.

"Yes, I am Hans Gruber," Hans replied.

"You have to report to *Hauptsturmführer* (Captain) Otto Schneider immediately," the young soldier said. Schneider was real soldier's soldier. He had been awarded the Knight's Cross of the Iron Cross, which was only awarded in recognition of extreme battlefield bravery and or successful military leadership.

"I wonder what that's all about," Sven said to Hans.

"I don't know but I had better go find out," Hans said as he crawled out of the foxhole and began to walk away then turned back to face Sven and said. "Try to behave while I'm gone and stay away from sharp objects, apparently you can't be trusted with them," Hans said then gave Sven a taunting smile and walked away.

Hans knocked on the door to Captain Schneider's office. "Come!" Shouted a voice from inside the room. Hans walks into the room with the captain.

"Captain, I am Corporal Hans Gruber reporting as ordered," Hans tells the captain.

"Hmm, I just don't understand it," the captain said.

"What's that, Captain?" Hans asked. "You have orders to report to Bad Tolz immediately for officers training. The orders are from Reichsfuhrer Heinrich Himmler himself. How the hell do you know Himmler?" the captain asked Hans.

"I don't," Hans replied. "I just ran into him one time in Berlin."

"Well you must have made a hell of an impression on him. You're going to be an officer. Get your gear together. There is a train leaving at twenty one hundred for Germany, be on it. Here are your orders. Heil Hitler," the captain said in a rush.

"Heil Hitler," Hans replied and quickly left the room.

Hans quickly made his way back to the foxhole and jumped down inside and sat on the ground in silence. Sven about to burst at the seams with anticipation asks Hans, "Well, what the hell is going on?"

"Himmler has ordered me to officers training at Bad Tolz," Hans tells Sven.

"Himmler? Have you lost your mind? Why would Himmler send you to officers training?" Sven asked.

"I don't know," Hans said. "I was in Berlin and I accidently ran in to the general and knocked him down."

"Let me see if I got this strait," Sven said to Hans. "You knock Reichsfuhrer Heinrich Himmler, general of the SS down and he makes you an officer?" Sven said in disbelief. "You are the luckiest bastard I have ever seen in my life," Sven said with a little bit of disgust in his voice. "You have got it all. A beautiful home, a marvelous wife, medals from two wars, and now they are going to make you an officer. Where am I? I'm sitting in the mud, filthy dirty in the middle of nowhere with a thousand

Russians who want to kill me and once again you are going on holiday," Sven said with a grunt.

"I have to be on the train at twenty one hundred," Hans told Sven.

"Tonight? You're leaving now?" Sven asked.

"The captain ordered me on the train and there is not much I can do about it. I am sorry I am going to leave you out here on the line again, buddy, I wish I could take you with me. I am going to worry about your dumbass," Hans said with affection.

"I will be just fine don't you worry. I just feel sorry for you, Hans, you're going to miss all of the fun. I heard it from a good source that the Russians are going to throw us a hell of a party in the morning," Sven said jestingly.

"Try not to have too much fun. I wouldn't want you to embarrass yourself in front of our Russian friends," Hans said to Sven as he pats Sven lightly on the cheek. "If you have to, get the hell out of here, Sven, don't be a hero. We have way too many of those as it is." Hans stresses to Sven. Hans opens his arms and he and his childhood friend embrace. Both men knowing that it could be the last time they see one another.

They both reluctantly release their embrace from one another and smile in love and in reassurance that they would one day reunite. Hans lightly slaps Sven in the face. "Dumb ass," Hans said to Sven. Hans shook his head, smiled at Sven then walked away. Sven stood there with his hand on his cheek from the sting of Hans's slap with a smile on his face, watching as Hans walked out of site. Sven then began to wonder if he would ever see his old friend again and his smile slowly faded away.

CHAPTER FOURTEEN

THERE WAS A HELL of a battle coming and Hans knew that his unit was outnumbered by both man and machine. The situation had never looked bleaker and Hans's mind was very troubled thinking about leaving his buddy just when he likely needed Hans most. Hans waited at the train station to board the next train back to Germany. He sat on a small bench beside the railway and began to think of his old friend and all the good times they had growing up together.

Hans thought of all the silly things Sven had done over the years and began to smile and chuckle to himself. Then he began to think about the new life he was beginning to start. Going to Bad Tolze and entering the SS officer's candidate school. Even though this opportunity would open a whole new world of opportunities for him, Hans still wondered to himself if it was the right thing for him to do. The excitement he should be feeling was overwhelmed with the concern he had with leaving Sven behind.

SS-*Junkerschule Bad Tölz* was an officers training school for the Waffen-SS. The school was in the town of Bad Tolz which is about thirty miles south of Munich. The location was chosen because it was in an inspiring location, both grand and beautiful. The design and construction of the school was intended to impress those that came to the training center and the local concentration camp Dachau provided labor for the center. The facility offered a number of amenities and the sporting facilities were second to none. The recruits had the opportunity to engage themselves in a number of different sports including football, skiing, and horse riding. As well as honing of the combat skills of the junkers or cadets the school's training also included lessons from basic etiquette to Nazi ideology. Some, like Hans, would take the ideological training with a pinch of salt, others were extremely dedicated to it. It was not good enough for the Waffen-SS officer to be an excellent military leader he had to be able to conduct himself properly in social situations with both superiors and subordinates as well.

The training was some of the hardest and it was designed to take each cadet to the very limit of their abilities. Much time was spent on field training and grueling cross-country runs, where each man had to carry a full load of combat weapons, gear, and ammunition. These runs were timed, and no one was allowed to fall behind. Continuous improvement and training to excel were emphasized with a heavy emphasis on camaraderie and teamwork.

The young officers were instilled that they were responsible for the actions of themselves and their men and that success or failure depended on them. They were to always participate as a member of the team and this was a distinct difference from either the wehrmacht or allied forces. Nothing else could compare to the mutual respect that was felt in all ranks of the Waffen-SS, from the senior officers down to the rawest recruit.

Waffen-SS officers were to lead from the front and always be in the thick of the action. The physical training was just one of the many things that would be covered at the academy and each candidate was given thorough training in the use and maintenance of a number of weapons. Though many of the candidates were familiar with some of these weapons, the training would give the candidates the opportunity to become familiar with many different weapons and the various tactical strategies that can be conducted with them. Though training for the men was excellent, even the best and toughest training program devised for the cadets by the Waffen-SS still could scarcely prepare them for the dangers and privations of the Russian front.

Hans boarded the train for Germany. Inside the car he saw a site that was almost as serial as battle itself. Hundreds of wounded German soldiers filled the cars of the train. It was the wounded from recent battles against the Russians. Hans wondered what horrors they may have seen and experienced. Luckily war was over for them, they would no longer see man's inhumanity to man, they were going home.

It was late and Hans was tired. He spotted an open seat near the middle of the car and sat down. Next to Hans sat an SS corporal. His head was all bandages and he was missing his left arm. Hans could tell the young corporal was in extreme pain due to the look of anguish on his face. Hans tried to start up a conversation with him to maybe cheer him up or just take his mind off the pain even if it's just for a little while.

"Looks like they got you good," said Hans to the corporal.

"They sure did," the young man replied. "Five hundred of us were assaulting a hill when a barrage of artillery from the Russians began to rain down on us. I was running next to my lieutenant when a shell came down right on us. The lieutenant was completely blown in half and I lost my left arm and right eye. Out of five hundred of us only forty nine of us survived." A look of fear and remorse came over both Hans and the corporal's faces.

They both looked at each other with empathy. "But I am going home," the corporal said with a smile that appeared almost to be a forced effort. The corporal slumped in his chair and a long breath exited his body. The boy no longer felt the pain of his wounds or visions of war in his head. He was free of the torment that had been bestowed on him.

Hans looked at the hand on the only arm the boy had left and saw a picture of a young woman and a baby. Hans took the photo from the corporal's hand and closely looked at it. He turned the picture over and on the back of the picture said, "Surprise, darling. You're a daddy to a beautiful baby boy. I named him after you, he looks just like you and he has a tiny nose and big ears just like daddy. Come home soon, darling, you son needs you."

Hans began to tear up and think about his wife. "Do I have a son?" Hans thought to himself. "Will I be able to go home and teach him how to fish and to be a man of honor and good morals?" Hans laid his head back on the top of the back of his seat. He continued to think about home and Carina back there waiting for his return. Hans had to make it back home to her and he was determined to do so.

At the break of dawn Hans was awoken by the sound of fifty caliber shells ripping through the train car and the wounded men's unsuspecting bodies inside. Holes the size of a man's fist was being created through the wounded men, it was as if parts of their bodies were exploding. The train was being strafed by a Russian fighter plane and Hans new he had to quickly exit the train as soon as he possibly could if he wanted to stay alive.

Hans stood up and began to run to the car exit door jumping over bodies that were ripped apart from the aircraft's deadly fire they were exposed to along the way. Hans made it out of the car door and steadied himself between the car he was on and the rail car in front of him. The train was still traveling down the track at a very high speed. Hans had to make a choice quickly. Do I jump off the moving train and possibly kill myself in the attempt or do I stay on the train exposed to the fifty caliber rounds that are slicing through both the train and the wounded inside like a hot knife through butter.

Before Hans could make a decision on what to do the train slammed on the breaks with a screech from the sound of metal upon metal throwing Hans into the car that was forward of the one he was on. As soon as the train came to a complete halt Hans jumped from the train and ran to a ditch about one hundred yards away for cover. Hans no sooner got in the ditch and looked back at the train and there was a loud explosion.

A fifty caliber round fired from the fighter penetrated the engine of the train and exploded with a force of an artillery round. The explosion jarred Hans and he began to think about Sven and the nightmare he may be going through right now. The feeling of shame came over Hans. He felt as he had deserted his childhood friend in an effort of gaining self-glory in becoming an officer in the SS. Selfishly leaving Sven fighting in the mud fighting the Russians that were bearing down on him.

Hans decided he could not leave his friend in great danger and live with himself while living the more pampered life as an officer. Hans had to go back to the front to fight and even die if necessary with his childhood comrade. His duty and dedication Hans had for Sven was much more important than a military commission so Hans decided to make the journey back to the front to share the same fate as his childhood friend.

Hans had walked along the railway for two days in an effort to return to his unit occasionally eating roots or raw potatoes from a farmer's fields. On the morning of the third day in the distance Hans spotted three tanks with men on top of them at an intersection of a dirt road and the railway. Hans could tell they were German but could not tell what unit they were with. Hans threw up his hands and frantically waved his arms in an effort to get the soldiers' attention. "Hey, hey, over here!" Hans yelled to the soldiers as he ran toward them.

The soldiers on the tanks heard Hans yelling in the distance and instinctively readies their rifles in defense from a possible attack, then recognizes him as one of their own. As Hans drew closer to the soldiers he could tell they were SS and began to feel a little more comforted. As he drew even closer he could tell that they were not only SS but Wiking SS and to his further disbelief it was the remainder of his own platoon. Albin was Hans's platoon sergeant and was standing on the top of the lead tank of the small Colum. Albin was a fellow Swede from Stockholm. He had joined the SS in 1940 when the Wiking group was first created before the invasion of Russia.

Albin looked the part of the perfect Aryan and was a firm believer of the Nazi ideology but he was generally a nice guy and a very cordial person. It was almost hard to believe this man truly believed in the annihilation of every Jew and Slav in Europe. That he thought that he was a true crusader in a war to rid the world of treacherous backstabbing sub-humans and that he was one of the new master race.

Though Hans thought Albin was a bit twisted in his beliefs he was overjoyed to see him. Hans ran to the side of the tank. He was exhausted, hungry, and severely dehydrated but he had made it back to his men. Albin bent down on the tank and outstretched his arm in an effort to pull Hans up to the top of the tank. "What the hell are you doing walking around out here in the middle of nowhere, where did you come from?" Albin asked Hans.

"I was on a train headed for Bad Tolze when the train was strafed and destroyed. That was two days ago and I have been walking ever since. Do you have any water?" Hans asked.

"Sure," Albin replied and handed Hans his half-filled canteen. Drink all you need my friend. Are you hungry?" Albin asked.

"I'm starving," Hans replied. Albin reached into his satchel and pulled out a Hartkeks, a German biscuit that was both hard and very bland tasting but it looked as appealing as a steak to Hans and he began to devour the biscuit.

Hans looked around as he tried to chew the cuisine that was graciously given to him and noticed that there we only a few men from his platoon on the tanks. "Where is the rest of the platoon?" Hans asked with a mouthful of tasteless biscuit ejecting small pieces out of his mouth as he talked.

"They are all gone, Hans. Out of thirty six men only fourteen survived," Albin said with remorse in his eyes. "We were overran this morning and had to get the hell out of there fast. I am not sure about the other platoons but we are all that's left of ours."

Hans looked around at the tanks in an effort to spot Sven but he was nowhere in sight. "What about Sven, where is he, did he make it?" Hans asked with a sound of desperation in his voice.

"Your buddy, he's fine, Hans, we sent him behind the lines to a medical facility yesterday. That's where we're headed now. We have more men here in desperate need of medical attention," Albin said with a reassuring smile. You will be able to see that maniac soon."

CHAPTER FIFTEEN

SVEN HAD A BIT of a reputation among the men. He was considered very brave, almost to the point of recklessness but the men truly respected and admired the man. He was also known as a bit of a practical joker and had a great gift for making people laugh. Hans thought the true reason Sven was like that was because he wanted the men to feel happy, at least for a little while in the middle of this hell they were in.

Hans knew Sven well. Sven pretended to be this carefree fearless and nonchalant man but Hans knew his deep empathetic and sensitive side of Sven even though he made a great effort to hide it from the world. As the tanks began to rumble down the dirt road, Hans thought back to a time when he and Sven were boys. Sven had this great idea to go around to the doors of people's houses and coat the door knobs to their front doors with butter. Sven thought this to be hilarious. Though he was never accused or punished for the crime everyone knew who had done it.

Even back home Sven had quite a reputation as a prankster. When people would see the two of them together they would greet Hans with a smile and lovingly rub him on the top of his head. Then they would turn their head to Sven and with half a smile shake their head and say, "And you, you little delinquent stay out of trouble." Then give him a little slap on the cheek. No one was ever mad at him for his deviant behavior. He somehow was just one of those people you just can't stay mad at and that was probably the only reason he stayed out of jail.

The remainder of Hans's platoon reached the small village where the medical facility was and stopped their tanks in front of the building. It was a church that had been recreated by the Reich to use as a makeshift staging hospital for the wounded. As soon as the tank stopped Hans jumped from the tank and hurriedly ran into the building in search of Sven.

Just inside the door was a nurse holding a clipboard. She was about four foot eight and look to Hans to be a hundred years old. Hans was immediately taken aback by what she was beholding. "What the hell is an old woman like that doing out here?" Hans thought to himself.

"Slow down, mister, this is a hospital not a racetrack!" the tiny woman bellowed.

Hans stopped in his tracks as the woman ordered him. His eyes grew big and his jaw dropped with a bit of a look of confusion on his face.

"Relax, boy, I'm not death, I am a nurse. What are you here for? Are you hurt?" the nurse asked with a bit of a scowl on her face.

"No, ma'am, I mean I am not hurt, ma'am I am just looking for a buddy of mine," Hans told her. They said he was wounded and sent here."

"What is his name, son?" the nurse asked.

"Sven Eriksson," Hans replied.

"Ah, Sven Eriksson," the nurse said shaking her head. "I am surprised that man has any friends. He has been nothing but trouble since he got here. He acts like a child and is disrespectful to my nurses."

"The sooner we get him out of here the better, I don't want him running off with one of my nurses, I need every one of them," the nurse said with frustration clearly in her voice.

"That sounds like my Sven, ma'am. I am sorry he has caused so much trouble, ma'am. It's rumored back home that his father hit him in the head too many times," Hans said with a crooked smile and a wink.

"Yes, I can clearly see that, perhaps he should have hit him a little harder," the nurse said returning a sarcastic grin. "Follow me and I will take you to him, just promise me you will take him with you when you leave," the nurse said as if she were asking for a favor.

"Yes ma'am," Hans replied and began to follow the nurse to Sven's cot.

Hans and the nurse walked over to Sven's cot. His body was covered with a blanket with only his head sticking out and he appeared to be unconscious. Hans kneeled down next to Sven. Hans felt terrible seeing his friend lying there wounded. Mentally punishing him for leaving his friend alone to face the danger he had gone through. If he were there perhaps Sven would not have been terribly wounded.

Hans gently shook Sven's arm in an effort to wake him. "Hey, old buddy, wake up," Hans said softly. Sven slowly stirred and realized it was Hans waking him. Sven quickly sat up on the cot with a huge smile on his face. "Hans, what are you doing here?" Sven asked happy to see him.

"The train I was on was strafed and destroyed so I came back here. Never mind me, how are you? Are you okay?" Hans asked with great concern.

"I am going to survive but I have been in great pain," Sven told Hans.

"I am so sorry, buddy. I should never have left you. How bad is it?" Hans asked with great sincerity. Hans was very worried that his dear friend had been morbidly disfigured from his wounds and would have to suffer the rest of his life with a disability he could never recover from. Sven pulled his left arm from under the blanket and held his hand up in front of Hans's face. Sven's pinky finger was wrapped in bandages from mid-point of his finger to the tip. Hans looked at the bandaged wound in disbelief. "I have been beating myself up for leaving you and worried to death that you had one foot in the grave and all because you were sent here for cutting your pinky finger?" Hans said with a little anger and disbelief.

"Hey, it really hurts. Besides, I didn't cut it, it was shot off. I will get a medal for this for sure," Sven said with a cheery and proud look on his face.

"You are an idiot!" Hans said angrily pushing Sven's hand away from his face.

"Hey, why are you back here? Shouldn't you be on you way to Germany for officers training?" Sven asked a little confused.

"I changed my mind. I don't think I want to be an officer. It's not where I belong. I am a farmer not an aristocrat," Hans explained.

"Are you crazy?" Sven asked in disbelief. "If I was offered an opportunity to become an officer I would jump on it," Sven said "You call me an idiot and that's the dumbest thing I have ever heard of. I think you just missed my pretty face," Sven said with a smile.

"I hate to destroy the delusion you have about yourself, Sven, but you have a face only a mother could love my friend," Hans replied sarcastically.

"Boy, I would have left your butt in the mud and not looked back. I am more of the officer type anyway. You're more of the country bumpkin type," Sven said.

"Why do I like you?" Hans asked shaking his head, just as he had asked himself a hundred times before. "Get your pathetic butt up and let's get back to our unit," Hans ordered Sven.

"Okay, just let me say goodbye to a couple of nurses before we go," Sven said with a look like the cat that ate the canary.

"Oh, no you won't, Romeo. I told the old dragon in charge I would get your pain in the butt out of here and that's what I am going to do. I am not going to stick around here and get my ass kicked by a little old lady just so you can flirt with some nurses! Now come on, let's go!" Hans said then started pushing his reluctant friend towards the door.

"How about I just say goodbye to one of them?" Sven asked with a touch of desperation.

"Not a chance, dumbass," Hans replied as he gave Sven another shove toward the door.

In the early part of 1943 the Wiking division was ordered to fall back. Hans and his men were to move as fast as they could to Ukraine, south of Kharkov to support divisions there. The fighting was fierce and they were up against the Soviet group Popov who were now threatening to break through the German lines and capture the vital rail line. The Russians had a heavy armored formation greatly outnumbering the German Panzer division.

Despite being outnumbered by Russian soldiers and tanks Hans's unit held back the Soviet assaults. The fighting was bloody and many times hand to hand. Hans and Sven were ordered to hold the line at all costs. From their position they could clearly see the center of town. The Russian brought out two SS men they had captured into the center of the street their hands tied behind them. They wanted to make sure that the Wiking division had a full and clear view of what was to happen.

The Russians then began to pour gasoline on the legs of the men. You could see the fear and desperation on the faces of the two SS men as they were screaming "No! Please no! For the love of God please don't do this!" One of the soviets bent down with a lighter and lit the pant legs of the SS men. The Russian had only doused fuel on the men's legs to make sure they didn't burn too fast. They wanted to make sure it was as painful and as horrifying as they could possibly make it.

The two men screamed in extreme agony as the flames slowly began to rise upon their bodies. After a few seconds the screams stopped and their charred bodies fell to the ground. One of the Russian men bent down over one of the still burning bodies. He proceeded to take a cigarette out of his shirt pocket and lit the cigarette with the fire from one of the bodies still burning on the ground. "Those dirty sons of bitches!" Sven said with rage and he began to stand to singlehandedly attack the Russians in an attempt of retribution.

Hans dropped his rifle and quickly grabbed Sven's leg tripping Sven and causing him to fall to the ground. Hans jumped on top of Sven to hold him down wrestling with him until he submitted to Hans's restraint. "Stay down you idiot, that's exactly what they want us to do so they can pick us off one by one with their snipers," Hans explained.

Sven came to his senses and they both low crawled back to their concealed positions. "I swear I would like to gut every one of those bastards like a fish," Sven said with a lust for vengeance.

"Pull yourself together and don't do anything stupid, I don't want to have to tell your mother you got yourself killed just because you had your head up your ass," Hans told Sven. Hans watched Sven for a little while. Sven began to stare at the ground. Somehow you could just tell he was thinking of how many horrible ways he could kill the Russians in an effort to avenge those two men so cruelly murdered by those heartless bastards. Hans thought to himself that in all the years he had known

Sven this is the first time he hasn't had a sarcastic comment to say about the situation. That childlike gleam he always wore on his face no matter what the situation was gone, replaced with a look of anguish and anger.

Hans's platoon sergeant came to their position with a young soldier. He was one of the replacements for the men that they had lost. He didn't look older than fifteen and Hans was sure that he most likely lied about his age to get in. "How old are you, boy?" Hans asked.

"Nineteen," the boy replied.

"What is your name, son?" Hans asked.

"My name is Wolfgang Schmitt," the boy replied.

"Well Wolfy, stick to our asses and do what we tell you and you might learn enough to keep yourself alive," Sven told the boy.

Albin hit Hans on the top of his helmet in order to get his attention. "We are moving out in the morning to take the rest of the town. You boys try to get some rest tonight but keep one of you awake at all times as a lookout. You never know when those sneaky bastards will attack," Albin told them. "Take care of him, he's just a pup," Albin said then gently squeezed the boy's shoulder and gave it a little pat as if he were talking to his son.

"These guys are the old timers of the platoon and they know how to not get their selves killed. Be sure and do what they tell you, okay, son?"

"Yes, Sergeant, I will," the young private replied.

"Well, I have to go to a briefing with the captain. See you assholes later," Albin said as he began to walk away.

"Such an eloquent man, I am surprised he is not an officer yet," Sven said with a hint of sarcasm.

Hans smiled and thought to himself. "Well I can see the old Sven is back."

CHAPTER SIXTEEN

TELL US A LITTLE about yourself, Wolfy," Sven told the boy. The young private began to tell them of home. How his mother loved to make pies and how he would sneak a bite or two when she wasn't looking. He said his father would get extremely mad at him for doing that but his mother always intervened and defended him. You could tell by the way the boy talked he loved his mother very much and she meant the world to him. "I joined so I could send money home. My father can't work. He fell off some scaffolding and broke his leg. He is a mason and very good at what he does. He is probably the best," the boy said proudly. Wolfy told them about his school days, all his buddies and that special girl back home he was determined to marry. Hans and Sven looked at each other and smiled. The boy reminded them of home and the life they had left behind. Both Hans and Sven somehow felt closeness to the boy and took a strong liking to him. Kind of like an adored little brother.

"All right, let's get some sleep. We are going to need all the rest we can get for the morning," Hans said. "Wolfy, you take first watch, Sven, take second and I will take third. If you hear something or you feel something is out of the norm, wake me up," Hans said to the young man.

"I will keep my eyes open," the private replied. Hans and Sven curled up to get a little sleep, morning would be there well before they would like it to be.

The next morning Hans woke Sven and Wolfy with a kick to their feet. "Wake up you two. It's time to assemble for the assault." The two sleeping men gave themselves a quick stretch of their arms and they were reluctantly on their way. The men received their orders and began to walk down the road toward the city square. Hans, Sven, and Wolfy hid at the side of a building with a few other men before turning the corner to the center of the square.

The SS soldier that was assigned to act as the point lookout slowly peeked around the corner of the building in an effort to see if there was any enemy defending the area. The soldier saw no Russians so he carefully walked around the corner of the building to the center of the street for a better look. Again the soldier saw no evidence of the enemy in the area. The soldier waved at the rest of the men that it was all clear and that they could proceed into the square.

As Hans was rounding the corner a short rang out from the other end of the square. A high powered rifle round pierced the chest of the point man throwing his body three feet back from where he stood. The round hadn't killed him and he was screaming in pain. There was nothing any of the SS men could do to help him. If any of them exposed themselves in an effort to save the young soldier they, too, would surely be shot and likely killed.

The man was screaming begging for someone to come help him. Another shot rang out and the bullet hit the wounded soldier in the leg causing even more pain. He screamed again from the pain of the round going through his leg. "We have to do something, I will get him!" Wolfy said and began to run out in the open to help the soldier. Sven quickly stopped him and said, "Stay here boy. I will take care of this."

Sven was an excellent marksman and always love the challenge of a hard shot. Sven lay on the ground and carefully looked around the corner. There was a church at the end of the square with a steeple on top. Sven figured that it was the most likely position a sniper would take and the right trajectory the bullets came from. Sven spotted a quick reflection of light from the center of a dark opening in the bell tower. Another short rang out from the sniper's rifle hitting the wounded soldier for the third time but this time in the shoulder.

Sven saw the rifle's flash when the sniper fired and he aimed his rifle directly at that point and fired. Seconds after Sven had fired a Soviet soldier fell from the tower to the ground below. "Super Sven strikes again!" Sven said boastingly. Hans looked at Sven and shook his head then rushed to the wounded soldier with a few other men. They reached the soldier but it was too late, he had already blead to death.

The men looked at the soldier for a few seconds in mourning then quickly got their composure to handle the job at hand. The men began to walk into the square. They split up into small groups to search the buildings for the enemy. Hans, Sven, and Wolfy entered the first building on the right. They entered the building and looked around inside. It looked as if the Russians were using the building as a command post. "Okay, look around to see if there are any maps or papers but be careful for booby traps," Hans warned them.

The three men began to look around and Wolfy spotted a large desk. It looked like a desk a commander would sit at so he walked over to take a look. On the desk was a box and inside the box were maps and other documents written in Russian. "Look what I found guys. It's a box full of maps and some kind of documents." Hans turned to look at Wolfy and to warn him not to pick anything up but before Hans could get the words out of his mouth Wolfy picked the box up to take over and show them what he had found.

Just as he lifted the box there was a loud explosion. Shrapnel and splinters of wood from the explosion went everywhere and the room filled with smoke and dust. Hans and Sven were thrown against the wall and then fell to the floor. Uninjured Hans and Sven tried to make their way to where Wolfy was standing when the explosion occurred. When the men got to Wolfy he was laying on the floor.

His head was gone from the eyebrows to the top of his head and both arms were blown off from the elbows down. They both looked at the boy in almost a state of shock. Wolfy's blue eyes were staring at the ceiling and he had a slight smile on his face as if he were seeing something very pleasant. There was dust and dirt on his face, Sven bent down brushed the dirt off the boy's face and closed his eyes.

Sven stood back up and looked at Hans. They both had tears in their eyes and began to cry for the loss of this young boy they had become close to so quickly. It was as if they had both lost a beloved family member. A little brother they had never had. Hans and Sven hugged each other to comfort and be comforted, they were all each other had in this madness. Another SS man stepped into the building. "Come on you two we need some help out here," the soldier said.

Hans and Sven quickly wiped the tears from their faces. They couldn't let another SS man see them cry. It was a sure sign of weakness and that was not tolerated in the SS. The men continued down the street toward the center of the square. They stopped for a moment in order to look around to make sure they would not walk into another sniper's field of fire. Hans and Sven stood in front of a two-story building, Hans's back to the door of the building.

A Russian soldier came barreling out of the doorway of the building with bayonet fixed to the end of his rifle in a suicidal attempt to kill any German he possibly could. With this in mind the Russian attempted to thrust his bayonet through Hans's back. The sudden movement of the Russian coming through the doorway caught Sven's attention and he reacted quickly to the danger. Sven raised his rifle and hit the Russian in the face with the butt of his rifle before the Russian had the chance to run Hans threw with his bayonet.

The Russian soldier fell to the ground unconscious. Sven quickly stood over the soldier straddling his body and began to pound the butt of his rifle into the face of the Russian soldier again and again. With each blow the soldier's face split open more and more and his skull began to be crushed from the repeated blows. Sven continued to hit the man's face over and over with his rifle even after it was clear that the man was dead. It was as if Sven had gone completely mad or perhaps it was his way of getting retribution for the death of young Wolfy.

Hans put his hand on Sven's shoulder. "Sven," Hans said trying to pull him back from whatever mental state he was in. Sven jerked his shoulder out of Hans's grasp and continued to hit the Soviet man's head with the butt of his weapon. By this time the Russian's face was unrecognizable as a human, just a mangled mess of flesh, blood, brains, and bone. Sven slowly stopped hitting the man and fell to his knees beside the Russian's lifeless body exhausted from his attempt for vengeance.

Hans put his hand back on Sven's shoulder. With a slight squeeze and a shake Hans said, "It's okay, buddy, it's okay. Let's go check out the building to see if there are any more of those bastards in there. The two men got to the entryway of the building and carefully peered into the room. It was dark, very little light but they could see enough to tell it was apparently clear of Soviet soldiers. Cautiously Hans and Sven entered the room, Hans in the lead followed closely by Sven.

As they both entered Sven looked to his right and saw the barrel of a Russian rifle pointed straight at his head. Sven immediately froze in place. "Drop your weapons," the Soviet soldier ordered. Hans quickly turned to see the Russian and raised his rifle in an attempt to kill him but before he could take aim he was hit in the head with the butt of a Russian rifle. The blow nearly knocked Hans unconscious and he dropped his rifle. Hans grabbed the Russian's rifle in an effort to wrestle it away from him but he was week from the blow to his head.

Hans and the Russian fell to the floor still wrestling for the rifle. The Russian overpowered Hans and sat straddled atop of him pushing his rifle into Hans's throat with all of his weight. Hans pushed back with both hands on the rifle with all his might but it was to no avail. The realization that he was going to die in that dark room was very clear to him and as his strength faded away he began to accept his fate. As Hans released pressure from the rifle accepting his demise, so too did the Russian.

"Hans?" the Russian said both questionably and with surprise. Hans opened his eyes and strained to look into the face of the Russian soldier that was just about to end his life. Hans's eyes grew big, in shock of what he was seeing. It was Borya, the Russian soldier he had helped to escape months earlier. "Hans, it is good to see you my friend," Borya said stretching out his hand in an effort to help Hans off the floor.

"You call this SS pig your friend. I will report this and you will be sent to a concentration camp in Siberia for this," said Borya's Russian comrade. He was a commissar for the communist party. Nothing gave the man greater pleasure than turning a fellow soldier in to the Russian KGB for being a traitor to the communist party. Even for voicing a negative opinion against the regime in any way. "Shoot him!" the commissar ordered.

Borya raised his rifle and aimed it at Hans, then quickly turned and aimed his rifle in the face of the Russian commissar and pulled the trigger. The round went into his face and exploded out of the back side of his head. Blood and brain matter spattered one of the white walls of the room as well as a painting of an old woman carrying wood that hung slightly tilted to the right on the wall. Hans and Sven looked at each other in disbelief.

"I never liked that guy. He was always such a pain in the ass," Borya said shaking his head. "I would love to chat with you, Hans, but you have to get the hell out of here. There are eight Russian soldiers on the second floor and if they see you, you two are dead men."

"You need to get the hell out of here as well, Borya. We are making a major push to take the city and it's not likely we will be taking prisoners."

"Thanks for the advice, Hans, now get out of here before one of them comes down and discovers the both of you," Borya said with true concern.

"Keep your head down, Borya, remember you still owe me a drink after the war," Hans said with a smile.

"I think we are even now but I will buy you that drink anyway, my friend," Borya replied returning the smile.

Hans said, "Good luck, my friend" shook Borya's hand and made his way toward the door. Hans and Sven both carefully look out the door to make sure it was safe to exit the building. Just before exiting Hans looked back at Borya one last time and gave him a smile. Borya returned the smile and gave Hans a quick wave goodbye.

CHAPTER SEVENTEEN

HANS AND SVEN SLIPPED out the door hugging the side of the building as they continued down the road toward the square. As the men were leaving a German Tiger tank came around the corner headed their direction. Seeing the Tiger gave Hans and Sven a little sense of security. Having a Tiger tank around as backup was a major deterrent to the enemy. The Russian soldiers on the second floor of the building just began to open fire and throw grenades at the tank.

The Tiger raised its eighty eight millimeter gun and aimed it at the building it was receiving fire from. The tank fired one round into the building causing a huge explosion. The two-story building collapsed into a pile of rubble. There was no doubt in Hans's mind that no one inside the building could passably survive such devastation. Hans was hurt, losing another friend but his thoughts took him to the drink they had planned to have together after the war.

Hans truly would have liked to have that drink and sit with Borya and talk about their war experiences together. Thinking about how he would enjoy that time with Borya gave Hans a little smile on his face. Then the reality of losing his friend came back to mind and the smile he had on his face faded away and his thoughts turned to sorrow. Hans and Sven continued their assault into the center of the square.

The boys reached the corner of the next street and Hans slowly peeked around the corner of the building. A Russian T-34 tank accompanied by twelve Russian infantry men were headed their direction and they had to get out of there quickly. "There is a T-34 heading this way, we got to get the hell out of here," Hans said to Sven with urgency in his voice.

"Shit!" Sven replied and the two men quickly ran back to the building the Tiger had just destroyed to conceal themselves amongst the rubble.

The T-34 rounded the corner and spotted the Tiger sitting on the road in front of the T-34 a block away and came to an immediate stop. The Russian soldiers dropped to the ground and laid all around the tank in an attempt to conceal themselves the best they could. The German tank commander standing out of the turret on top of the Tiger spotted the Russian tank and immediately dropped down inside the tank to inform the crew of the impending danger.

The barrel of the eighty eight millimeter gun on the Tiger was facing the left side of the tank pointing down a side street. The gunner of the Tiger tried to traverse the barrel forward to fire at the T-34 but the turret would not traverse due to the barrel of the gun being blocked by the corner of a building. The T-34 fired at the Tiger but the round bounced off the three inches of armor on the front of the Tiger tank.

Albin ran in front of the Tiger to direct it backward waving to the driver in an attempt to clear the building and fire at the T-34. "Go back about three feet!" Albin yelled to the driver in an effort to clear the barrel from the building blocking its traverse. The T-34 fired at the Tiger a second time. The round from the T-34 hit the front of the left side track of the Tiger with a huge explosion immobilizing the Tiger from moving forward or back.

The concussion from the explosion threw Albin into the radiator at the front of a burning truck killing him. The explosion destroying all of his internal organs from the pressure wave created from the detonation of the round. The gunner of the Tiger tried to traverse the turret forward one more time in a desperate attempt to put a round into the T-34. The barrel of the eighty eight millimeter gun clipped but broke through the corner of the building as the gunner attempted to swing the gun around.

Before the T-34 could get off the third round, the Tiger fired at the T-34. The round hit the T-34 between the body of the tank and the turret throwing the turret of the T-34, fifty feet straight up into the air destroying the tank killing all inside and many of the Russian troops that were around the tank. One of the surviving Russian soldiers attempted to make a hasty retreat. Before the man could get to his feet, the turret from the T-34 drops from the sky crushing the soldier then bounces off him ending up on its side leaning against the front of a bakery.

The remaining four Russian soldiers quickly retreated down the same road from which they came in a desperate effort to save their own lives. It became deathly quiet. The Russians were now in full retreat. The men of the Wiking regiment were exhausted and still under strength from the fighting in the Caucuses. Though they lacked sufficient armor to counter the Soviet force, the division held off the Soviet's assaults protecting the rail line and insuring the destruction of mobile group Popov.

After recapturing Kharkov, the Wiking division was pulled back from the front to be refitted as a Panzergrenader division. An elite mechanized infantry division consisting of half-tracks to transport the infantrymen and a well welcomed increase in Panzer tank strength. During this transformation into a Panzergrenader division, Hans and Sven were given a well-earned leave to go home and visit their families they had not seen in such a long time due to the desperate need for men on the Russian front.

Hans, Sven, and several other comrades from SS Wiking boarded a train heading for northern Germany. You could feel the excitement in the air on the train of the men about to return home to their loved ones. The men were all as giddy as schoolgirls joking, laughing, and giving playful taunts to one another. It was a joyful relief from the constant fear, horror, and chaos of the war. As the train pulled away from the station, the soldiers settled down into their seats.

The car Hans was on became quiet but Hans noticed as he looked around at the other men, all of them had smiles on their faces as they all were thinking how wonderful it was to finally go home. A few of the men got together to play cards to alleviate some of the boredom of the train ride but most of the men leaned back in their seats in order to get some peaceful sleep. Something that is almost impossible to have on the front while constantly worrying that every snap of a twig was a Russian trying to sneak up on you to slit your throat.

In the early hours before dawn the train pulled into a railway station, the slowing of the train and the screeching of the wheels on the tracks waking the men from their slumber. When the train came to stop Hans and the rest of the Wiking men noticed a strange sounds coming from the train next to them. Hans and several other men in the car lowered their windows to see if they could clarify what they were hearing.

The men poked their heads out of the train windows and heard hundreds of men calling out for help. Women were wailing and children crying and there was a terrible stench of feces, urine, and death that was almost to the point of being overwhelming. The men could see arms outstretched through the slits in the top of the enclosed cars, their hands stretched open as if trying to desperately grasp some type of salvation from their horrific situation.

Hans spotted a guard for the train with the human cargo that was walking between the railcars. "Hey!" Hans shouts trying to get the attention of the guard.

"What?" the guard replies with a bit of a grumble.

"What is going on here, why are all these people on this train like that?" Hans asked.

"They're Jews, what do you think?" the guard said sarcastically.

"Are they being relocated or something?" Hans asked without a clue of what was going on.

"Right," the guard replied. "They are headed to their new home at Auschwitz. These dirty vermin won't be a problem to the Reich much longer."

Hans noticed that the soldier was Einsatzgruppen SS, a soldier in Hitler's death squads. Hans clearly knew what that meant having seen their special talents being put to use before. Hans looked down the railway. There seemed to be hundreds of rail cars stretching off into the distance until out of view from the darkness. There must have been thousands of Jews on the train. Hans sat back down in his seat with a look of fear, confusion, and disgust on his face. How could a man have a lack of conscience and morality to do such a thing? Hans wondered. To kill a man in battle is one thing, to kill innocent men, women, and children because of their religion is another.

"Hey, buddy," Sven said shaking Hans's shoulder. "Don't think about it. We are going home. Think about your sweet little bride and all the dirty little things you're going to do to her when you get home," Sven said with a perverted grin on his face.

"Shut up asshole, that's my wife," Hans said with a bit of a scowl on his face.

"Sure, pal, you're going to be a perfect gentleman with her when you get the chance to be alone with her. You're going to be like a dog in heat and maybe you will do some of the sick and perverted things I would do with her," Sven said nudging Hans with his elbow. "Boy, if I had the chance," Sven said then Hans cut him off in mid-sentence.

"You're not going to get the chance. Now sit down and shut your mouth you idiot before I pop you one in the jaw," Hans said to Sven holding his hand in a fist in front of Sven's face.

"Yeah, the poor girl doesn't know what she is missing not having a guy like me to take care of her needs and being stuck with a prude like you," Sven said slapping Hans's fist away from in front of his face.

Hans rolled his eyes, sat back in his seat, and shook his head. "Why do I like this guy?" Hans asked himself as he has done a hundred times before.

Sven said as he snickered, "It's because you love me, sweetheart." Sven then wiggled around in his seat trying to find a position that he was comfortable in then closed his eyes and attempted to get a little more sleep.

As the train continued down the track, Hans tried to think of home and Carina but his mind kept drifting back to the people calling out and wailing on the train they saw at the station. What misery and torment they must be going through. Hans thought of the poor little children not understanding the hell they were going through and wondering why these bad men were doing this to them. The more Hans thought of it the more his eyes began to fill with tears. Hans believed in what he was doing, fighting the spread of communism but began to wonder which was worse, Hitler's fascism or Stalin's communism.

Hans began to question himself on how he could possibly fight one evil and fight for another. Hans looked out of the widow at the full moon in the night sky as a tear slowly rolled down his cheek. Was Hans one of these bad men by association? Was his reasoning for being in this war truly sound? These thoughts began to become heavy on his mind. Hans had never felt more troubled than he did at that moment. The excitement and joy of going home was taken over with both shame and confusion. The weight of worry in his mind on what he should do was overpowering his feelings of happiness in his thoughts going home.

CHAPTER EIGHTEEN

AFTER A LONG AND exhausting railway trip Hans and Sven made it to Sassnitz in northern Germany and took the ferry to Trellborg, Sweden. The excitement of both men was growing large in the thoughts of surprising their families, neither of which knew they were coming home. The drive from Trellborg to Osby was only a couple of hours. Soon the boys would be home to a very familiar and heartwarming place, far from the war.

Hans and Sven walked to the bus station not far from where the ferry had dropped them off. They bought tickets home and sat down at a bench to wait for the bus home, they had a thirty minute wait. Hans noticed a young Jewish couple with a beautiful blonde little girl with pony tails. The girl was about six years old and had a smile that would light up a room and raise anyone's spirits with her gentle innocence.

The girl smiled at Hans and gave him a timid wave hello. Her eyes were as blue as the sky and reminded Hans of Carina's mesmerizing eyes. Hans thought how lucky she was to be here and not back in Germany where they would surely take her and her family to a death camp. Hans felt as if he owed her something, some type of payment for the sins of the Einsatzgruppen's actions back in mainland Europe. Hans walked over to the small concession stand the bus station had and bought a chocolate bar for the little girl. Hans took the bar to the little girl's father. "Sir, may I give this to your daughter?" Hans asked with a smile.

"Yes," the father said and Hans leaned over to the little girl and said, "Here, sweetheart, I hope it brightens your day as much as you have mine" and handed it to the girl.

The girl hesitated for a moment and looked at her father for approval. Her father nod his head yes and she timidly took the chocolate from Hans. Shyly with a smile she looked at Hans and said, "thank you, sir."

"Thank you, that was very kind of you," the girl's father said to Hans with a smile.

"No need to thank me, sir, I think it brings me greater joy than it does her. It's been a long time since I have seen a beautiful little face like hers, she warms my heart," Hans said to the girl's father.

"What's your name?" the girl asked in a tiny voice.

"My name is Hans, what is yours?"

"My name in Gina," the girl said. "I love chocolate."

"Me too," Hans said with a smile, and then walked back to the bench where he had been sitting before.

A few minutes later Gina and her family were told that the bus to Stockholm was ready to board. Gina's mother and father stood up. "Come, Gina, it's time to go," said her father. Gina stood up and quickly ran over to Hans and gave him a hug.

"You should come to my house someday, my mommy is a good cook," Gina said to Hans.

"Okay, Gina, I will. Have a good trip, sweetheart," Hans said with a loving smile.

Gina ran to her mother and took her hand. "Goodbye, Hans," Gina said with a smile and a wave as she and her parents walked away. Hans watched Gina and her parents walk away with a warm and loving smile. That little girl had given Hans the greatest joy he hadn't had in a long time. The only greater joy he had ever experienced was the day he finally got to marry the love of his life, Carina. The short time spent with this beautiful little girl was a touching moment Hans would never forget.

A man's gruffly voice came over the bus station's loud speaker. "Now boarding for Osby," the man said. Sven gave Hans a light back handed swat on his arm. "Come on, buddy, we are almost home," Sven said with a smile. Hans smiled back at Sven and they both jumped to their feet and walked over to the bus to board. The two men climbed aboard the bus and made their way to the backseats and sat down.

Soon the bus pulled away from the station and they were on their last leg of the trip home. Ten minutes into the trip the bus slowed down to a stop. Hans heard gasps coming from the front of the bus "Oh my God!" One woman at the front of the bus shouted. Hans and Sven both stood up and leaned forward in an effort to look out of the front windshield to see if they could spot what all the commotion was about.

There was a train stopped on the tracks blocking the road and a mangled bus lying on its side almost ripped in half about a hundred feet from the right side of the road. Many of the men of the bus Hans had been traveling on began to quickly exit the bus in an effort to possibly help those who were injured from the accident including Hans and Sven.

All of the men ran toward the mangled bus checking each one of the bodies that had been thrown about from the violent rolling of the bus for any signs of life and injuries. Hans looked around and noticed the body of a man lying facedown in the dirt. On the man's head was one of those little round hats the Hebrews wore called a kippot. Hans bent down over the man and rolled his body over. It was the father of that beautiful little girl Gina that he had met at the bus station.

Hans stood up and ran around the grizzly seen desperately searching for the little girl that Hans instantly felt so close to back at the station. "Gina! Gina!" Hans yelled out as he scurried around. "Gina, where are you, sweetheart?" Hans yelled again.

"Hans!" Sven shouted trying to get Hans's attention. She is over here, Hans."

Hans ran over to the girl. She laid there lifeless, her pretty little lace lined dress covered in blood and her little innocent eyes staring into the clear blue sky. Hans knelt down next to the little girl. He put one hand under Gina's head and the other on her back and pulled the lifeless girl into his arms and embraced her. Hans began to rock back and forth with her and began to cry uncontrollably. Sven knelt down next to Hans and put his hand on his devastated friend and began to cry as well. Hans released the girl from his loving embrace and gently lay her back on the ground. Hans looked over the girl from head to toe and noticed one of her shoes was missing from her foot. It was one of those little black shoes with a silver buckle and a bow on the toe of the shoe.

Hans looked around but did not see the shoe. Sven knew what Hans was looking for and began to look around as well. Sven spotted the shoe a few feet away and walked over to get it. "Here it is, Hans," Sven said as he handed Hans the shoe. Hans took the little shoe from Sven and began to undo the tiny little silver buckle, then gently raised the little girl's tiny foot to put it back on for her.

Hans began to look around and he spotted the bus driver standing in the middle of the carnage with a dazed and confused look on his face but relatively unscathed from the accident. Hans stood up and wiped the tears from his eyes then walked over to the bus driver with Sven following close behind. "What the hell happened?" Hans asked the bus driver.

"We were a little behind schedule. I saw the train coming and it seemed to be going rather slow. I didn't want to have to wait for it to pass and be even further behind schedule so I stepped on the gas to get across the tracks before the train came. I guess I must have had a little misjudgment on the time I had to cross the tracks."

"You had a little misjudgment?" Hans said angrily. "All of these people died because you had a little misjudgment? You stupid son of a bitch! I am going to kill you!" Hans said angrily and he then grabbed the bus driver by his collar and threw him to the ground. Hans straddled the bus driver and began to hit him over and over in the face.

The bus driver whimpered and attempted to cover his face with his hands in an attempt to protect himself from the blows from Hans's fists. Sven grabbed Hans's arm to refrain him from beating the bus driver to death. "No, Hans, this won't bring her back, buddy. Let's go," Sven said to Hans as he pulled Hans up and away from the driver.

Hans walked back to the little girl's body and gently picked her up into his arms. He walked back to the road with the girl in his arms softly speaking to her as if to try and comfort the little girl.

Hans sat down in a spot of green grass next to the road with Gina still in his arms. Hans sat there for hours rocking the girl, talking softly to her as he ran his fingers through the little girl's long blonde hair until help arrived to take the injured and the dead away. Once the train was pulled further down the tracks, clearing the road so the bus could continue the journey, all of the passengers boarded the bus. The bus pulled away from the deadly crash site and as the bus continued down the road the only sound heard was the rumble of the engine of the bus. Not a word was spoken by the passengers the rest of the way to Osby.

Many of the passengers wondered how something so terrible could happen to innocent people, while others just pondered their own mortality. Hans, emotionally devastated, anguished in the loss of a little girl who had stolen his heart. The bus reached the Osby bus stop late in the afternoon and the boys still had quite a bit of a walk home and it would be dark by the time they got there.

"Do you mind if I spend the night at your house tonight? I am feeling a little wore out after the day we had," Sven asked Hans with a yawn.

"Sure, you can stay in my old room tonight. Just try to keep a low profile tonight I want to spend a little time alone with Carina," Hans said to Sven.

"Oh, I understand, my friend," Sven said with a wink and a smile. Just let me get a little something to eat and I will be right off to bed."

"Thanks, buddy," Hans said as he patted Sven on the shoulder.

CHAPTER NINETEEN

THE BOYS REACHED HANS'S home just at sunset and Hans knocked on the door. They smiled at each other in the joy and anticipation of surprising Carina. "One moment, please." The boys heard the sweet and familiar voice from the other side of the door. Carina opened the door and her eyes grew big and the shock of seeing Hans was overwhelming.

Carina fainted and fell to the floor just inside the doorway hitting her head on the door knob. As she fell Hans said, "Oh shit!" as he and Sven both reached out in an attempt to catch her from falling at the same time to no avail. Hans bend down and picked Carina up and carried her in his arms to a chair in the front room.

"That's our Carina," Sven said with a hint of sarcasm. "Graceful as a ballerina, I see she hasn't changed."

"Shut up, Sven, she could be hurt," Hans said with concern for Carina.

"I have no doubt about that," Sven said. "She wouldn't be Carina if she wasn't somehow hurting herself."

Hans looked up at Sven as he tried to revive her with a scowl on his face. "You're an ass," Hans said to Sven. Hans held Carina's head as he looked her face over and brushed back her hair to see her forehead where it had struck the handle of the door.

Carina had a small bump on her forehead about the size of a nickel, other than that she was just fine. Carina came to and saw Hans's face. She quickly grabbed Hans, her hands holding his head covering his ears and began kissing him all over his face like a starving person devouring bread they had just been given. "Hans, you're finally home!" Carina said with excitement.

"Yes, I'm home, sweetheart. Are you okay? Hans asked with concern.

"I have never been better, Hans," Carina replied with a smile of immeasurable joy from ear to ear.

"I am sure she is fine. She should be used to falling down by now. She has done it about a million times since we have known her," Sven said with a smile.

"Sven, your home too, it's so good to see you. I see you haven't changed either, still as mischievous as ever," Carina said as she shook her finger at Sven.

"Sven is going to stay the night tonight and go home in the morning. Is there anything to eat, honey, we haven't eaten all day," Hans asked.

Carina grabbed Hans by the head again and gave him several more kisses on the face. "Sit down at the table, boys, and I will fix you something to eat," Carina lovingly told them.

"How is your family?" Hans asked Carina.

"Mama and Papa are fine. They will be so happy to see you. Papa always asks how his favorite son-in-law is doing," Carina said as she sliced the bread for the sandwiches she was making them.

"It's good to know that I am his favorite considering I am his only son-in-law," Hans replied.

"Now don't be silly, you know Papa loves you very much. He couldn't love you any more than if you were his own son," Carina said sincerely.

"I know, sweetheart, I love him too. Very much so, he has always been like a second father to me," Hans replied.

"Yes he loves you very much and is very proud of you. He worries about you quite a bit fighting at the front like you are. I worry too, have you seen a lot of terrible things at the front, Hans?" Carina asked with worry and fear on her face.

Hans walked over to Carina and from behind her Hans put his arms around Carina. "No, darling, it's not near as bad as one would think. Let's not talk about the war, I am here to be with you," Hans said as he hugged her with a tender squeeze and a little kiss on her cheek.

Carina turned around to face Hans, still in his embrace. "I am so glad you are home, I love you so much," Carina said and then gave Hans a long passionate kiss.

"Okay, enough of that you two, can't you at least wait until I go to bed to do that?" Sven said with a slight frown on his face.

Hans and Carina both turned to face Sven and gave him a little smile and a giggle. "Oh, do you two remember my cousin Elsa? She is coming to visit me for a few days. Isn't that wonderful?" Carina said in anticipation of her dear cousin's arrival. The boys vaguely remembered Elsa. The last time they saw her she was about twelve. Hans and Sven both remembered that Elsa was a skinny little girl with freckles and a bit of an overbite and she got great joy in tattling on them for anything they did wrong. "Oh god, not Elsa, I can't stand that little witch," Sven said with a cringe thinking of her.

"Hey, she is a wonderful girl and I want you to stick around so you can say hi to her," Carina demanded.

"Okay," Sven said as he rolled his eyes and shook his head.

"Hey, don't complain," Hans told Sven. "I have this sinking feeling she is going to be staying in my house while she is here."

"That's right," Carina said, "and you're going to be nice to her. You two got that?"

"Yes," Hans and Sven reluctantly said as if they were children being scolded by their mother. Carina brought the sandwiches and sat them both down on the table. "You two sit down and eat while I put new linen on the beds," Carina said as she walked into the other room to grab fresh linen.

Hans and Sven ate their sandwiches. They tasted wonderful, so much better than that army swill they had been forced to eat for so many months. The boys finished their sandwiches and leaned back in their chairs. "God that was good, I have missed this so much," Hans said patting his stomach.

"Oh me too," Sven replied. "The beds are ready, boys!" Carina yelled from the other room.

Both men jumped up out of their seats and headed for their rooms both excited to sleep in an actual bed instead of a dirty foxhole. The boys got to the room Hans had as a child. "Here you go, buddy, have a good night," Hans said to Sven.

Sven looked into the room and saw the bed with clean sheets and they were already pulled down for him to crawl right in, it looked like heaven. "Oh, I will have a good night, but I am sure not quite as good as yours. As tired as I am right now it will be close enough for me. Good night," Sven said then eagerly entered the room closing the door behind him.

Hans walked down the hall to his and Carina's bedroom. Carina was just inside the door to greet him. Carina put her arms around Hans's neck and gave him a passionate kiss. "I am going to make you forget all about that war tonight," Carina said with a devilish smile and a seductive tone. "Get in bed, sweetheart. I will be right back here in a minute to give you something special." Hans's face gleamed with anticipation, and quickly took off his cloths and crawled into bed. The bed felt wonderful to Hans. He hadn't laid on a bed this soft since he left home and it felt so warm and relaxing.

A few minutes later Carina walked into the room with a smile on her face. "You are going to love . . ." Carina stopped mid-sentence and the smile faded from her face. Hans was lying in bed, mouth open and snoring. Carina shook her head. "I can't believe this," she said with a slight and understanding smile. She didn't have the heart to wake Hans so she carefully crawled into bed and snuggled up to him. "I have waited this long, I can wait one more night," Carina thought to herself. She then closed her eyes. Feeling the comfort and warmth of Hans's body next to hers, it quickly and serenely put her fast asleep.

The next morning Carina was up before dawn preparing breakfast for her favorite two men, Hans and Sven. Cooking for the two men brought her great pleasure after being alone for so long. Carina decided to fix a good hearty breakfast the likes of which she was sure they had not had in a long time. The breakfast was more of a traditional Swedish breakfast that they would not have had the opportunity to have down in mainland Europe.

Carina fixed her boys smorgas, an open faced sandwich consisting of bread, butter, and a slice of cheese. She also spiced up the sandwiches with *gurka* (cucumber), *tomat* (tomato), and *skinka* (a cold cut made of ham). Carina prepared the breakfast, set the table, then woke Hans and Sven to come to breakfast and eat. The men slowly and groggily walked to the dining table. When they saw what Carina had prepared for them their eyes opened wide and a joyful smile immediately came to their faces.

"This is wonderful, Carina, thank you," Hans said gratefully.

"Damn, Hans, you are so lucky. I wish I had a woman like Carina waiting at home for me," Sven said with envy.

"Sorry, buddy, I got the last one," Hans said as he turned to look at Carina giving her a smile of love and gratitude. The men finished breakfast and began to talk about what they would do while home on leave.

A knock came from the front door and Carina walked over to see who could be coming to the house this early in the morning. Carina opened the door to see who it could be. "Elsa!" Carina yelled and then walked out the door to greet her. Hans and Sven still sitting at the table looked at each other and rolled their eyes in dread of having to see this unpleasant gangly girl that they luckily had had not seen in years.

Carina stuck her head in the doorway "Boys, come say hi to Elsa. Come on in, Elsa, I have a wonderful surprise for you. You will never guess who is here." Hans and Sven got up from the table and walked into the adjoining room toward the front door. Carina grabbed Elsa by the hand and pulled her into the house.

As Elsa entered the room both Hans and Sven stopped dead in their tracks, their jaws dropping nearly to the floor from the sight they were both beholding. Elsa was unbelievably beautiful. She was literally the ugly duckling that grew up to be a beautiful swan. "Okay guys, you can close your mouths now," Carina said.

Hans shook his head. "Elsa, I can't believe it's you. The years have definitely been good to you. You're like a flower that has blossomed. You're definitely not that awkward little girl you used to be," Hans said in amazement. There was no reply from Elsa and the room was silent. Hans and Carina both looked back and forth between Elsa and Sven. They both were staring at each other. Hans and Carina looked at each other. It was very clear to them that both Sven and Elsa were smitten with each other. Hans and Carina continued to look at both of them not quite believing what they were seeing. Neither of them had ever seen Sven react this way to any woman, it was totally out of his character and seeing this beautiful woman responding to that irresponsible goof Sven the same way was almost unfathomable.

As if no one else was in the room Sven walked toward Elsa and took her hand. "It's wonderful to see you after all these years, Elsa, come with me and tell me how you have been," Sven said to Elsa as he led her out of the room to the dining table to talk. Elsa willingly and even eagerly complied with Sven and followed him into the other room still holding on to Sven's hand. Hans and Carina still stood there in the living room both of their faces covered with disbelief and confusion at what had just taken place.

Sven and Elsa sat at the table and talked for hours. It was clear to Hans and Carina that this was defiantly a case of love at first sight but they were still bewildered at the actions of the both of them. Sven, the supreme womanizer, the man of whom the only woman he had ever treated with respect was his mother, this not to be confused with behaving her. Now behaving as an obedient lap dog, hanging on to every word his loving master speaks.

Then there was Elsa, a refined and beautiful woman willingly submitting herself to the control of a man that Hans and Carina knew as the most irresponsible and depraved ding-a-ling they had ever known. Perhaps there was something they saw in each other that they each needed. Who could say, love is a baffling emotion of which no one can control. "Hey, I know you two don't realize or even care that there is anyone else in the house but what do you say we all take a little day trip down to Osby lake? It's a beautiful day and I don't want to stay inside all day, let's get out in the sun and breathe some fresh air. We can take a picnic basket with us and just spend the whole day there," Carina asked with built up enthusiasm and excitement in her face.

"That sounds like a wonderful idea Carina, let's do it," Elsa said looking at Sven holding his hand with a beaming smile.

"That sounds like a lot of fun, let's do it," Sven said surprisingly.

Hans leans over to whisper in Carina's ear, "This has got to be love, when Sven agrees to spend the day doing something that doesn't involve beer and loose women that's all it can be," Hans said sarcastically. "The world is surely coming to an end."

Carina giggled and slapped Hans on the chest. "You're a wonderful man, Hans, and I love you very much but romance is certainly not your forte."

"Not my forte?" Hans asked. "When have you ever known that man to ever be romantic?"

"Never judge a book by its cover, Hans. You never know what wonderful things may be hidden inside. Now, go get a blanket out of the closet that we can lay on the ground to sit on and I will put some food and plates in the basket for us. Go on," Carina said as she slapped Hans on the butt to get him moving.

"You're the boss," Hans replied as he walked down the hall to retrieve the blanket he was ordered to get.

CHAPTER TWENTY

THE TWO COUPLES ARRIVED at Osby Lake and Carina picked out just the right spot under a large tree that provided plenty of shade with a beautiful view of the lake. "Hans, spread the blanket out over there under the tree," Carina said pointing at a nice grassy area.

"Boy, you sure have gotten bossy since the last time I saw you," Hans said grumbling under his breath.

"Someone has to be in charge, Hans, and I thought it over long and hard, and I chose me," Carina said with a stern look on her face that quickly turned into a smile and a giggle.

"I guess I can live with that," Hans said as he spread the blanket on the ground.

"Does this spot please you, my love?" Hans asked Carina with a smile and a wink.

"Yes, that's fine, now go get the box with the wine and the glasses out of the car," Carina ordered.

Hans began to walk to the car to retrieve the box. As Hans passed Sven and Elsa who had been standing nearby watching the comedic sparring between the two, Hans looked at Sven, then Elsa, and then back at Sven. With Hans's eyes open wide shaking his head Hans whispers, "Don't get married." Sven and Elsa look at each other and laughs out loud.

"What did he say?" Carina asked the giggling couple. "Hans, you are just asking for troubles, aren't you?"

Hans turned his head and smiled back at Carina as he continued to walk to the car. Carina smiled and said "I love you" without making a sound from her voice. Hans stopped at the car and replied to Carina by blowing her a kiss.

Sven turned to Elsa, both having seen the loving affection Hans and Carina gave to one another. "I never thought I would say this, Elsa, but God I want that," Sven said to Elsa, the words coming from deep in his heart.

"I do too, Sven," Elsa said leaning closer to Sven. Sven leaned down and gave Elsa a tender and gentle kiss then he and Elsa stood there staring into each other's eyes.

Hans and Carina looked at each other still not believing what they were seeing. Sven has never acted this way. It was if he were a completely different man from the one they have known all of these years. Elsa had put some kind of spell on Sven. He behaved with loving affection. He was sincere and respectful to Elsa. All of which were traits Sven had never displayed before.

The two couples had a wonderful and relaxing day at the lake and the temperature was perfect, not too hot and not too cold. The sun was out. There were white fluffy clouds floating by and a beautiful blue sky that seemed to go on forever. They could not ask for a more delightful day. "Oh, Sven, there was something I forgot to tell you," Carina said.

"What's that?" Sven asked her.

"Your mother and father are out of town until next Sunday, they went to go visit your uncle in Stockholm. Apparently he is in bad health," Carina told Sven.

"Is he going to be okay?" Sven asked very concerned for his uncle. Sven's uncle was ten years older than his father and seemed to always be in bad health, he was the sickly one of the family. Sven's father, on the other hand, was the "oops" baby.

His father had eight brothers and sisters, apparently his grandmother could not keep his grandfather away from her. She seemed to be in a constant state of pregnancy until the ten year break between the birth of his uncle and his father. The family joke was that his grandfather had either been too tired from raising all those children to get frisky with his grandmother during that time or that he was away for ten years.

"No, they think he is going to be fine. He had caught pneumonia but he is getting better. Your mother suggested that they go so that they could help take care of your uncle, but your father said that he thinks it's just an excuse that she is using so that she can go to Stockholm and do some shopping."

"That sounds like mom," Sven said jokingly. "Since mom and dad are away would you like to stay at my house, Elsa? I have plenty of room and I am sure that Hans and Carina would love a little alone time together," Sven asked Elsa.

"That cunning rascal," Hans thought to himself. "Sven had figured out a way to get Elsa alone with him at his house and made it sound like that he was doing a good deed and being very considerate to Carina and I." Sven had always been as cunning as a fox with women. It was if he could be with a woman for ten minutes and he could convince them to go to bed with him, clearly a skill that he had inherited from his grandfather.

"That's a great idea, Sven, I am sure they would love the chance to discover one another again," Elsa said.

"Great, let's go," Sven said as he quickly stood up.

"Hold on, big fella. We are all having dinner at my house first. I am going to fix us all something special, then you can go home," Carina authoritatively told Sven.

"Yes, ma'am," Sven replied. "I can't turn down your meals, Carina."

Carina was a great cook. She had spent her childhood cooking in the kitchen with her mother and had learned every secret recipe that had been handed down from generation to generation from the matriarchs of her family and the boys having grown up with her knew that very well. "Okay then," Carina said. "Let's get everything together and we will head home, I don't want dinner to be too late."

"I will give you a hand, Carina, it will be fun cooking something together," Elsa said excitely.

The girls put the dishes in the basket then Carina folded the blanket. Hans and Sven had just been standing there looking out at the lake while Carina and Elsa had been gathering their things. Carina picked up the basket and blanket then forcefully handed them to Hans. "Here, make yourself useful," Carina ordered.

"I am just a pack horse to you, aren't I?" Hans asked.

"Yes, Hans, yes you are. That's why I married you, I needed a good mule to move thing about the house," Carina said then they both smiled at each other and headed toward the car.

Once the couples arrived back at Hans's house, Carina and Elsa got right at preparing dinner. Hans and Sven decided that they would tinker around the car while the girls were working in the kitchen. "So, I gather you like her?" Hans asked as if he wasn't sure about Sven's feelings for Elsa.

"Oh yeah, I do," Sven said nodding his head and raising his brows with eyes open wide. "I know you probably couldn't tell but I like her a lot."

"Wow, Sven, I never would have known," Hans replied as if he had not a clue.

"Yep, that's why the call me pokerfaced, Sven."

"I can see why they would call you that," Hans said turning his head to look at the car's engine so Sven could not see him rolling his eyes. Hans and Sven piddled around on the car for about an hour, just killing time while waiting for the evening's cuisine that Carina and Elsa were preparing.

Carina yelled out of the front door to Hans and Sven letting them know that dinner was ready. "Come in and get cleaned up, dinner is ready," Carina said with a smile. She was excited for the boys to see what she had worked so hard preparing for them and was bursting at the seams in anticipation. Hans and Sven washed their hands and walked into the dining room.

They both saw what lay before them on the dining table and could not believe their eyes. It was as if they had died and gone to heaven, they hadn't seen anything remotely like this in months. "Oh my god, Carina, this looks wonderful!" Hans said not believing his eyes.

"A woman as beautiful as she is and can cook like this too, you are the luckiest bastard I have ever met, Hans," Sven said with unquestionable envy.

Carina had made a dish called *Janssons frestelse* (Jansson's temptation). It's a creamy potato and anchovy casserole mixed with potatoes, onions, anchovies, and cream, a Swedish favorite and quite a treat.

This was followed by a desert called semlor. It is a cream bun that is very lightly sweetened, cardamom-scented bun. It is filled with a creamy almond paste and topped with a generous swirl of fresh whipped cream. It is a mouthwatering treat and it is usually served with coffee or tea. Carina was both beaming with pride for the pleasure she gave to Hans and Sven and grateful to have the opportunity to do so. She had spent many months alone waiting for Hans to return home. The joy she felt being able to cook such a fine meal for others after making very simple meals for herself to eat alone felt wonderful and gave her great pleasure and satisfaction. The couples sat down at the table and began to eat the lovely dinner Carina provided for them. Hans and Sven began to devour their food like someone was going to steal their dinner from them.

The boys were not used to a relaxing dinner and had forgotten how to eat like civilized men. They had spent too long on the front where you have to eat your meals quickly due to the danger of having your attention taken away from the fight too long. A sure way to get you and your buddies killed. "Hey, you two, don't eat like pigs," Carina demanded. Hans and Sven looked at each other not understanding what Carina was talking about.

Eating like that had become the norm to them. Hans thought about it and realized that he was eating like a pig and that he didn't have to, there was no danger here. "I am sorry, Carina. I guess we are just not used to eating like a normal person anymore. All that time on the front has made us forget our manners," Hans tried to explain.

"I understand, sweetheart, and I am sorry too. I hate that you have to live like that and I hate you being gone and I hate this damn war too!" Carina said as her voice grew louder and more upset as she spoke.

CHAPTER TWENTY-ONE

CARINA BEGAN TO CRY uncontrollably and she quickly got up from the table and ran to the other room. Hans and Sven were both confused by this sudden outburst of emotions and sat there with dumbfounded looks on their faces. Elsa looked at the boys with a scowl on her face and said, "Idiots." Then got up out of her chair and ran to the other room after Carina.

"What the hell was that about?" Sven asked Hans still confused at what had just taken place.

"I'm not sure," Hans replied. "Did I say something wrong?"

"I don't think so, I didn't hear you say anything that might be upsetting," Sven replied still confused. "I tell you what, buddy, women look sweet and they are nice to have around sometimes but I think every damn one of them is crazy," Sven said utterly convinced of his reasoning.

"I can't disagree with you, my friend, there are many times I wonder about that myself. I remember even mom would flip her wig every once in a while about something and you know as well as I do Carina does," Hans said. Elsa walked back into the room. "I think you two should stay the night at Sven's house tonight, Carina and I need to talk," Elsa ordered.

"Wait a minute, I don't . . ."

Elsa put her hands on her hips, raised her eyebrows and gave Hans a death stare cutting him off in mid-sentence.

Hans raised his hands to surrender. "Okay, okay we will go to Sven's house."

Elsa walked back out of the room to go and comfort Carina. "You dumbass, you don't know when to keep your mouth shut, do you?" Sven said to Hans with a snarl.

"Don't give me that crap, you don't know what I said wrong either," Hans replied.

"I had that beautiful woman coming to my house tonight and you screwed it all up," Sven whined to Hans.

"Shut up, stupid, she's too good for you anyway," Hans said.

"I know that and you know that, but she didn't know it and now there is not a chance in hell of that happening. Thanks, buddy," Sven told Hans.

"Shut up and let's go," Hans said.

The boys started walking toward the front door. "Hey, let's take the desert with us," Sven said.

"Good idea," Hans replied and they both quickly walked back to the table and grabbed their desert plates, then both of them scurried out the front door. Hans and Sven walked down the dirt road to Sven's parents' house, eating their deserts as they walked. "Wow, this is fantastic!" Sven said. "I will have to thank Carina for this tomorrow. You know, if you hadn't opened your big mouth and upset Carina you could have thanked her properly tonight, Hans."

"Shut up, you don't even know what I did wrong," Hans said as he kicked dirt from the road at Sven.

"I may not know but you better figure it out and apologize for it. I want Elsa at my house tomorrow night so don't screw it up," Sven said. "Hey, you want to get drunk tonight? I bet dad has some cognac and beer at home, he always does," Sven asked with a devilish smile.

Sven's dad was a drinker, he wasn't quite an alcoholic but he did love his spirits. As typical boys, when they were young they would sneak sips of Sven's dad's cognac and beer out of his kegs. Sven's dad caught them sneaking drinks a couple of times but they never really got in trouble. Sven's dad would yell at them. "Hey! You two delinquents stay the hell out of my beer!" Like he was going to beat them to death but as they would run away the boys would turn around and see him laughing about it, thinking that they were just boys being boys so to speak.

Sven's mother, on the other hand, had caught them once and there was "hell-to-pay." The boys made damn sure not to get caught by her again.

"Why not," Hans said. "That sounds kind of fun." Hans and Sven reach Sven's home. They entered the door and Sven went straight for the liquor cabinet. Sven opened the door to the cabinet and looked inside. "Well, well, well. Look what we have here. Two brand new bottles of cognac. A virgin has to give it up sometime, shall we pop her cork?" Sven said with a smile.

"Sven, you are sex fiend. All the years I have known you, since we were just boys everything has been about you either trying to get sex or talking about sex. It's as if you're obsessed with it, why is that?" Hans asked with a desire to be enlightened.

"Now that hurts me deeply, Hans. I am not obsessed with it and I resent that accusation. Everyone needs a hobby that just happens to be mine," Sven said in his twisted attempt to clarify why he was the way he is.

"You are a lost cause, my friend. Now pop that bitch and pass her over," Hans said with a smile.

"Now that's my boy," Sven said with excitement in his voice and that ornery smile on his face like he had when they were kids when Hans would agree to go with him and steal sips of his father's liquor. Hans and Sven sat around drinking and talking about old times for hours.

As it grew late into the night the boys felt jollier and jollier. They broke out into an old Swedish drinking song called *Helan Gar. Helan* (the whole) is an expression signifying the first (small) glass of spirits in a series, and går means goes (down). Completely inebriated they stood up while singing the song and put their arms on each other's shoulders and walked outside into the front yard.

While standing in the yard singing, Sven fell to the ground and passed out lying on his back. Hans started laughing at Sven. With slurred speech Hans said, "You're a lightweight, what happened to you?" He continued to laugh at Sven then said, "Okay, okay, I will help you up." Hans reached down and picked up Sven's hand. "Come on, buddy," Hans said and then tried to pull him up. Sven's weight was too much for Hans to lift under his drunken condition and Sven's weight pulled Hans to the ground as well. Hans lay on his back and laughed. "Oh boy, I think I am drunk," Hans said laughing then passed out on the grass lying next to Sven.

The next morning Carina and Elsa had been waiting for Hans and Sven to show up at the house. Most of the morning had passed and at eleven o'clock Carina was becoming worried. She wondered if Hans was angry with her for being upset the previous evening. Perhaps she had hurt Hans's feeling and he didn't want to come back.

Carina called Sven's house and there was no answer of the phone. She was all a fret. "If the boys wouldn't make it here by noon we are driving over to Sven's house to find them," Carina told Elsa.

"Okay, honey," Elsa said to Carina as she put her arm around Carina's shoulder in an attempt to comfort her. Everything will be okay, you will see," Elsa said trying to reassure Carina.

Noon came and went. Hans and Sven still hadn't shown up at the house. "Okay, Elsa, let's get in the car and drive over to Sven's house," Carina said to Elsa.

"Okay, sweetie, let's go," Elsa replied. The girls got in Carina's car and drove over to Sven's house all the while worrying that she had possibly hurt Hans's feelings and that he didn't want to see her because he was angry with her.

Carina pulled in and parked in front of Sven's house. "Oh my god," Carina said fearfully. Hans and Sven were lying motionless in the front yard and Carina was worried that something terrible had happened to them. The girls quickly got out of the car and ran over to where the boys were lying. Carina grabbed Hans's head and lifted it. "Hans, Hans, are you okay?" Carina said frantically.

Hans came too and immediately grabbed his head in pain. "Not so loud," Hans moaned. "My head feels like it's going to explode."

Carina could smell the liquor on Hans's breath. "You bastard, you were drinking and passed out on the lawn!" Carina said very angrily at Hans. "I have been worried to death thinking the worst and you're passed out from a drunken binge!"

Carina angrily pushed Hans's head back down to the ground. "Ow, damn, Carina, that hurt," Hans said holding his head in agony from the hangover.

"You deserve that, you idiot!" Carina said then stood up and stormed back to her car. The girls got back in the car and in a fit of rage Carina stepped on the gas very hard peeling out throwing rocks and dirt from the road out behind her as she drove away.

"Looks like you screwed up again, Hans," Sven said holding his head in pain as well.

"Shut up," Hans said to Sven. "You know you have been getting me in trouble our whole lives, why do I let this happen?"

"Hey, don't blame me, buddy, you're a big boy now, you make your own decisions," Sven replied proclaiming his innocence in the cause of Hans's trouble.

"Shit, what am I going to do now? I'm in big trouble," Hans said as he sat up still holding his head.

"I don't know," Sven replied. "All I know is you're making me look bad in front of Elsa." Hans took his hand and grabbed Sven's face and pushed Sven back to the ground. "Come on, dumbass, let's get cleaned up and figure out what we are going to do," Hans said.

"I'm not sure what that would be but you better think of something good, she's pretty mad," Sven groaned as they both struggled to stand up, then stagger to the house.

The boys got themselves cleaned up and began to brainstorm for a while, trying to figure out what they could do to get back into the girls' graces and get themselves out of the trouble they were in. Hans and Sven sat down at the kitchen table to throw each other some ideas over a cup of coffee. "Okay, Sven, do you have any ideas?" Hans asked, not having a clue on what do to about the situation they had gotten themselves into.

"Flowers," Sven said as if he had discovered the lightbulb. "The first thing we need to get is flowers."

"Where are we going to get flowers?" Hans asked.

"Old lady Eriksson's house, on the way over here I noticed that she had a lot of roses in her front yard. She will never miss them if we only take a few," Sven said.

"Not a bad Idea," Hans replied, a little shocked that Sven actually came up with a good idea. "We can grab a few of them on the way back to my house. Now, what can we tell them?" Hans asked.

"Well, let's see," Sven said. "Oh, I got it!" Sven said excitedly from having yet another eureka moment. "We tell them that you were so sad and hurt from the pain you had caused her that we decided to have a drink and think about what you had done and what you could do to help make it up to her for your inconsideration and lack of sensitivity. We could tell her one drink just led to another as you were feeling so ashamed at the way you treated her and took her for granted that before you knew it we were drunk."

"Perfect, you sneaky bastard. How do you come up with this stuff?" Hans asked, not having the devious skills that his old friend had.

"I have had years of practice, buddy, and believe me, it has gotten me out of plenty of trouble," Sven proclaimed proudly.

"Somehow I can believe that," Hans told Sven. "Okay, let's get it together and head over to my house."

CHAPTER TWENTY-TWO

HANS AND SVEN HEADED out the door with smiles on their faces and despite the hangover a little pep in their step. They were sure their diabolical plan would work on Carina and get the both of them out of trouble. They headed down the old dirt road toward old lady Eriksson's house to commit their deviant crime. There was on old oak tree close to old lady Eriksson's house and Hans and Sven hid behind to conceal them. The boys peeked around the tree to make sure that the coast was clear. Old lady Eriksson was nowhere in sight. "Okay, let's go," Sven said and the boys ran into old lady Eriksson's yard as if they were assaulting a hill back on the front. They quickly picked a couple of flowers off the rose bushes that old lady Eriksson's took such meticulous care of. A shout came from the house. "Hey, you two!" yelled old lady Eriksson.

"Shit! Let's get out of here, Hans!" Sven said and the boys ran out of the yard and down the road with their ill-gotten booty as fast as they could. When out of sight of old lady Eriksson the two men fell to the ground at the side of the road panting from their sprint and rolling around on the ground laughing about the childish crime they had just committed. It reminded them of the days of their youth so long ago and the mischievous things they were always doing. "Wasn't that great?" Sven asked still chuckling from their deed.

"Just like old times," Hans replied.

"God, I miss those days," Sven said remembering the nostalgia of days gone by. "Oh, I do too, buddy," Hans said as he slowly stopped laughing and began to

mentally reminisce of their youth, wishing it had never ended.

Hans and Sven reached their destination and Hans, feeling a little odd about it, knocked on his own front door. The door opened, Elsa answered the door and stood there in front of them with a scowl on her face. "Ah, it's you two idiots. You know you two are in big trouble," Elsa told them.

"I know and we are sorry. Can I please talk to Carina?" Hans asked Elsa.

"I'm not so sure she wants to talk to you," Elsa said looking down her nose at Hans.

"Please, Elsa?" Hans pleaded.

Elsa rolled her eyes, "Hold on, I will see if she wants to talk to you." Elsa turned her head looking back into the house. "Do you want to talk to him, Carina?" Elsa asked.

There was no sound and Hans and Sven looked at each other a little worried. After a few seconds of silence they heard Carina say, "only if he is here to apologize for being such a jerk." Elsa looked back at the boys giving them the stink eye. "Okay, you two, you can come in," Elsa said then opened the door half way and walked back into the house and stood next to Elsa. Both of the girls stood there, arms crossed with angry looks on their faces.

Hans leaned over to Sven and with desperation in his voice whispered, "Shit, I forgot what I was supposed to say."

Sven put his hand on Hans's shoulder and with a slight cringe on his face said, "I guess you are on your own, pal."

"Gee, thanks, buddy," Hans said with clear sarcasm and they meekly walked in the door. They both stood in front of the girls with flowers in their hands. These two petite little women putting more fear in Hans and Sven than any Russian soldier ever had. Hans held out the rose in front of Carina to give it to her in an effort to break the ice a little. Carina quickly snatched it out of Hans's hand and recrossed her arms, glaring at Hans with a stone face.

"I am sorry, Carina, I didn't mean to hurt you. You know how guys can be very stupid when it comes to emotions and things," Hans said trying to explain. "You have known me my whole life and you know that I would never intentionally hurt you. I am so sorry, Carina. Tell me what I can do to make it up to you?" Hans said with sincerity clearly in his voice.

Carina stood there quietly for a second then looked over at Elsa then back to Hans. Carina unfolded her arms and held her hands together in front of her. "I know you didn't mean to, Hans, I know that guys are just idiots," Carina said. "You two have shown me that time and time again over the years."

"I love you, Carina," Hans said to her.

"I love you too, Hans," Carina said then walked over to Hans and gave him a forgiving hug and kiss.

Watching the love and forgiveness between Hans and Carina that was unfolding before them, Elsa and Sven looked at each other with smiles on their faces. Sven stuck out his arm presenting to Elsa the lovely red rose he had stolen for her. Elsa gratefully took it from Sven's hand and followed suit giving Sven a forgiving hug and kiss as well. Sven and Elsa decided to go to Sven's house to give Hans and Carina the privacy and alone time they had so desperately needed. Hans and Carina spent the rest of the day making love and being intimately playful with each another, something that they had not been able to share for such a long time.

Around 1:00 p.m. the next day, Hans and Carina were just cleaning up after having lunch when a knock came at the door. Hans opened the door and to his surprise it was Sven and Elsa. Sven had a grin on his face that went ear to ear and Elsa was just beaming. "Where is Carina? I have something to tell her," Elsa asked immediately.

"Uh, she is in the kitchen," Hans told her with a confused look on his face.

Elsa pushed her way through the door and rushed into the kitchen where Carina was washing dishes.

"What's going on?" Hans asked Sven.

"Hurry, let's get in the kitchen," Sven said as he also pushed through the door rushing toward the kitchen.

Confused, Hans closed the door and quickly stepped into the kitchen to find out what was going on.

"Guess what happened this morning, Carina," Elsa said ready to explode with excitement.

"What happened?" Carina asked just as confused as Hans.

"Sven asked me to marry him, and I said yes!" Elsa exclaimed.

"Oh my god!" Carina yelled as she and Elsa grabbed each other's hands and began to jump up and down giggling like two little school girls.

Hans's jaw dropped to the ground and his eyes grew as wide as silver dollars. He looked at Sven in total confusion and disbelief at what he had just heard. Sven stood there with a goofy grin on his face nodding his head. "I did, Hans, can you believe it?" Dumbfounded Hans replied, "Uh…no…I…uh…I don't," he said looking like a dear in the headlights. Hans put his arm around Sven's shoulder and directed him in the other room so that the girls wouldn't hear their conversation. "Are you sure this is what you want to do, have you really thought about this?" Hans asked with concern thinking that Sven was not being rational in his decision.

"Yes I have, Hans. She is the only woman who has ever made me feel complete. She is the only girl that has given me the desire not to be with other women and only to be with her. I'm in love with her, Hans. I have never felt as wonderful as this ever before."

"I have known you a long time, buddy, and I have never seen you like this with any girl before so I guess this must be love. Congratulations, Sven," Hans gave Sven a warm hug and patted him on his back, "I love you, buddy, I hope you will be as happy as Carina and I have been."

"You're not going to kiss me are you, Hans?" Sven asked jokingly.

"No, Sven, I can tell you didn't shave this morning and you know I don't like the feel of the stubble on my skin," Hans replied with a smile.

"You always have been the sensitive one, Hans."

"Come on, Sven, it sounds like the girls have their composure back so it might be safe to go back into the kitchen. Let's get us some coffee."

"Hey, is there any of that semlor we had for desert left?" Sven asked.

"Yes, I think there is," Hans replied.

"Great, I love that stuff," Sven replied. The boys went in and sat down at the table and talked while Carina started a pot of coffee for them.

"So, you two, when's the big day?" Hans asked.

"Tomorrow," Sven replied.

"Tomorrow," Hans said a little surprised.

"Yes," Elsa said. "We want to do it as soon as possible. Will you two come to the court house tomorrow and stand up with us?" Elsa asked.

"Of course we will, Elsa. You don't even have to ask. I would be as mad as hell with you if you didn't though," Carina told her.

Hans and Sven looked at each other with crooked smiles. "It must be a girl thing," Hans said laughing as the words came out of his mouth.

"Shut up you two and eat your semlor," Carina ordered. "Oh Elsa, we have to go shopping. You two better be sober when we get back or the wedding is off!" Carina bellowed at the boys with a warning of imminent doom on her face.

"Are you talking about my wedding, Carina? Wait a minute I . . ." Carina cut Elsa off by sticking her finger up in front of her lips.

"Quiet," Carina said to Elsa then turned to the boys and shook the same finger at them as a warning. Carina grabbed Elsa by the hand and they both ran out the door giggling and talking about what they were going to buy. Hans and Sven smiled and shook their heads then began feasting on their semlor that they loved so well, savoring every delicious taste.

Later that evening Carina and Elsa returned from their shopping expedition. As expected, they had to model every piece of clothing they had purchased to Hans and Sven. The boys quickly noticed that the girls, like typical women, bought a lot more clothes than they needed or intended to buy. This, of course, forced Hans and Sven to suffer through what they thought was a long and grueling display of clothing that neither had any interest in whatsoever but being a good loving husband and a husband to be, they acted as interested as they possibly could for the women they loved.

The girls displayed every bargain that they had acquired during their shopping spree to the boys. The only article of clothing Hans and Sven were spared was the dress Elsa had bought for their wedding the following day. Though it wasn't going to be an extravagant traditional wedding, Elsa wanted to keep as many traditions as possible in the wedding that they were to have. Elsa had something old and something new. Something borrowed and something blue. She also wanted to keep the tradition of not allowing the groom to see the bride's dress before the day of the wedding. The dress wasn't a white flowing gown but it was beautiful and that was just fine with Elsa. As far as she was concerned, even if she had to wear a gunnysack to the wedding in order to marry Sven, she would gladly do it. Elsa was in love with Sven as deeply as a woman could ever be. It was if she had a magical spell cast upon her but Elsa didn't care, she felt more wonderful than she had felt all her life and it was all because of Sven.

"Okay, you two you need to get out of here now," Carina told the boys. "Hans, you're staying at Sven's house tonight."

"What?" Hans and Sven both asked at the same time with the same confused look on both of their faces.

"That's right, Elsa and I have a lot to do to get prepared for tomorrow."

"But I want to sleep in my own bed tonight," Hans said whining like a child to Carina.

"You two just do what you're told, Elsa can't spend the night with the groom the night before the
wedding. It's just not proper," Carina said in a scolding tone.

"That's crazy, we just spent last night together," Sven said not quite comprehending the logic of the two women.

"You two just hush up and do what you're told," Carina ordered. "The wedding is at ten in the morning, I expect you both to be there on time and you better stay out of trouble tonight. Now get going, you two, we have things to do."

"Yes, ma'am," Hans said to Carina.

Hans and Sven reluctantly stood up and headed for the door. "Boy, she sure has gotten bossy since you two got married," Sven told Hans.

"You noticed that too huh," Hans replied.

The boys headed out the door and once again down the old dirt road they both knew so well. "I hope Elsa doesn't get as bossy as that after we get married," Sven said to Hans.

"Oh, she will be, buddy, believe me," Hans said convinced in his belief. "They all do and you can't fight it either, no matter how hard you try you just won't win. It's just one of those things us guys just have to accept whether we like it or not."

"Damn, Hans, maybe I should rethink this," Sven said. "It's too late now, buddy, your ass is already in the frying pan," Hans said as he put his arm around Sven's shoulders as they continued walking down that old dirt road.

CHAPTER TWENTY-THREE

THE NEXT MORNING HANS and Sven arrived at the courthouse at nine thirty in the morning to make sure that they wouldn't be late. Hans noticed that Sven looked a bit pale and a little nervous. "Damn, Sven, you look as if we were assaulting a Russian tank back at the front."

"No, Hans, that's not as near as scary as this," Sven replied with a shaky voice.

"Relax, buddy, the worse doesn't happen until it's been a year so after your wedding, that's when you have an excuse for getting nervous" Hans said with a smile trying to make his old friend feel a little better about the new life that he was about to begin.

Hans and Sven walked into the building and found the office of the Justice of the Peace. The boys stopped at the door and looked at each other. "Are you ready, Sven?" Hans asked.

"I think so," Sven replied. Then he took a deep breath and exhaled as he opened the door to the office. Hans and Sven walked in the door and Carina and Elsa was already there waiting for them. Sven looked at Elsa and thought that she had never looked more beautiful than she did at that moment.

Elsa looked at Sven with a loving and welcoming smile and held out her hand to Sven to hold. Though Elsa didn't have a wedding gown she looked very elegant. Her dress was white and it sparkled in the light. Sven wasn't sure what the sparkles were but he didn't care, he was about to marry the most beautiful woman he has ever known. The Justice of the Peace had a piece of paper in hand. "Okay, all we need is for the happy couple to sign here," the Justice said.

Sven signed the paper then looked into Elsa's eyes with a smile. Elsa then signed the paper and when finished grabbed both of Sven's hands and held them in hers. "Congratulations, you're now married," the Justice said.

"Wait a minute, is that it, is that all there is?" Hans asked the Justice.

"Yes, that's pretty much it, son," the Justice replied.

"Oh, that's not going to work. Sven, Elsa, look into each other's eyes," Hans told the couple. The newlyweds looked into each other's eyes as Hans had told them to. "Sven, do you promise to love honor and cherish Elsa until death do you part?"

Sven gave Elsa's hands a light squeeze and with a loving and tender smile said, "I do."

"Elsa, do you promise to love honor and obey Hans until death do you part?" asked Hans.

"I do," Elsa said. "Except for the obey part, he is the one that better be doing the obeying," Elsa said jokingly.

"Can you live with that, Sven?" Hans asked.

"I will try," Sven replied.

"Okay then, with absolutely no authority at all I now pronounce you both husband and wife. You may now kiss the bride," Hans declared.

Sven and Elsa then gave each other a passionate and endearing kiss. Elsa then walked over to Hans and gave him a loving hug. "Thank you, Hans, that made my wedding very special and I will never forget it or you. You will truly forever be in my heart." Then kissed Hans on the cheek.

Hans's eyes began to tear up. He gave a heavy sniff and quickly dried his eyes.

"What do you all say we go get a drink to celebrate, I'm buying," Hans asked Carina and the new couple.

"That sounds great! I'm not one to turn down a free drink," Sven said. Even though it wasn't a grand reception, Hans was determined to make this an unforgettable night for the new bride and groom with music, dancing, and drink. Hans knew that the joy his best friend felt at this moment would soon be transitioning back into the horrors of war.

The days drifted by like a dandelion seed in the wind. It was time Hans and Sven had to return to their unit, back to the fighting Fifth SS. They had to go back to the desperate attempt of stopping the advancing Russian Army from invading Western Europe. Carina and Elsa drove Hans and Sven to Trelleborg, Sweden so that the boys could catch the ferry back to Rostock, Germany. The two couples reached the ferry in Trelleborg just in time. The ferry was leaving in ten minutes.

The two couples stood in the boarding area, both women in the arms of the men they love. The girls were crying but doing their best to keep their composure in front of the boys. They both knew that it was very possible that it could be the last time they would get to see them, and they wanted to hold them in their arms as long as they could. "Hans, please be careful, don't try to be a hero or do anything foolish. Promise me," Carina begged.

"Don't worry, sweetheart, I will be hiding behind Sven the whole time, I promise," Hans said with a smile.

Carina softly slapped Hans on the chest. "You silly boy, you have always known how to make me feel at least a little bit better when I hurt. Even when we were kids I would fall down and skin my knee, you were always there to pick me up, dust me off, and dry my tears. Even then I loved you. Come back to me, Hans, I can't make it without you," Carina begged as she cried and rested her head on Hans's chest.

"Hey, hey now, don't you worry. Look here at what I have." Hans pulled some old medals out of his left shirt pocket. "Do you know what these are?"

"Yes, of course. They are your old medals that you were awarded back in the Winter War of '39," Carina replied.

"That's right," Hans said. "I keep these with me at all times, they are my lucky medals. As long as I keep these nothing bad will ever happen to me, I promise."

Carina looked into Hans's eyes. "I love you, Hans."

"I love you too, sweetheart," Hans replied giving Carina a warm, loving, and reassuring smile.

A call to board the ferry came over the loud speakers. It was time for Hans and Sven to leave and they both said their last goodbyes and kissed their wives. The boys boarded the ferry and went back to stand on the stern of the boat. Hans and Sven waved goodbye as the ferry pulled away from the dock. "Be sure to write, as soon as you can!" Carina yelled to Hans.

"I will," Hans replied and he blew her a kiss.

Hans and Sven stayed back on the stern of the boat until the girls were out of sight. Carina and Elsa both stood on the dock as well occasionally waving until the boys could no longer be seen by them. Once the girls were out of sight the boys looked at each other and smiled but the smiles were not those of joy but more of an understanding of each other's pain in leaving the women they love. Hans put his arm around Sven's shoulder. "Let's go inside and get us a seat," Hans said to Sven then both of the men walked somberly inside the ferry.

January through February 1944, SS Wiking took part in The Korsun Shevchenkovsky Offensive and led in the Battle of the Korsun Cherkasy Pocket. There was furious fighting around Cherkassy and the Wiking SS suffered heavy losses. Even though they suffered devastating defeats at the hands of the Russians their morale and espirit de corps remained high.

The Russian Army encircled the German forces of Army Group South in a pocket near the Dnieper River and during the weeks of fighting, the two Red Army fronts surrounding the Wiking unit tried to eliminate the remainder of the men of Wiking once and for all. The encircled Wiking units attempted a breakout of the pocket with other German forces and the fighting was fierce and bloody, again suffering heavy casualties and the loss of many desperately needed tanks.

Hans and Sven weren't sure they were going to make it out of this one, the situation was bad and their future looked very bleak. They were sure that there was a very likely chance that they would end up dead or shipped to a concentration camp in Siberia, the latter of which was doubtful. It was well known to the men that the Russians didn't take SS men prisoners. They were usually shot on sight in retaliation for the brutality the Einsatzgruppen SS had committed against their people behind captured German lines.

This was very callas but Hans thought it was probably well deserved from what he had seen the Einsatzgruppen do to innocent men, women, and children. The weather was bitterly cold and the men were quickly running out of food and ammunition. As many Junker JU 52 cargo planes that could land on the makeshift landing field they had created would land and take as many of the wounded as they could possibly carry.

The Junkers were slow lumbering aircraft and easy targets for the Russian anti-aircraft weapons. Just after lifting off the ground with a load of wounded on board one of the Junkers was hit in the wing of the aircraft blowing the left engine off the wing of the plane. The aircraft spun in and crashed about a hundred yards away from Hans and Sven's foxhole. The aircraft caught fire and the wounded men inside on stretchers were trapped inside the burning aircraft.

Hans and Sven could hear the screams of the wounded men as they slowly burned alive. As usual Sven tries to jump out of the foxhole in a foolish attempt to save the doomed men aboard the burning plain. Hans quickly grabbed Sven by the ankle as Sven reached the top of the foxhole. "Get your ass back here you idiot, you're going to get yourself killed!" Hans yelled as he strained to pull Sven back into the foxhole by the leg. Sven struggled to get loose from Hans's grasp but could not succeed in freeing himself.

Hans pulled Sven into the six foot deep foxhole that they had dug and Sven landed on his back at the bottom of the hole. Sven was rolling side to side in pain from the fall gasping for air as he tried to catch his breath from having the wind knocked out of him. Hans watch Sven rolling around in pain. "You deserve that, you idiot. There are Russians everywhere. You would be dead in three steps. How in the hell would I explain to Elsa that you got yourself killed trying to be some kind of hero. Now keep your ass down. I don't want her bitching at me because of your stupidity, I already have a woman to that I don't need two," Hans said scolding Sven as Hans kicks Sven hard on his leg.

Sven knew Hans was right. He has responsibilities now. Sven has a wife to take care of and to go home to, a real reason to live. "Sorry, Hans, I wasn't thinking," Sven said. "I would hate to have to put you through that hell," Sven said laughing.

"Just keep your ass down," Hans ordered. I need you alive so I will have somebody to hide behind when the shit hits the fan." That night there was a full moon out and it was very illuminating. It was dark but you could clearly see between fifteen and twenty feet away. In the darkness just out of sight a voice shouted out, "Patrol coming in, don't fire!" Hans and Sven looked at each other, both with confused looks on their faces. "I never heard about any patrol going out tonight," Hans said to Sven.

"Advance, slowly," Sven ordered the patrol. The soldiers from the patrol came just into sight of Hans and Sven. "Halt!" Sven again ordered the patrol.

Hans, Sven, the two SS men dug into the left of them and the two men on their right got out of their foxholes and carefully with rifles at the ready, walked over to where the patrol was standing. It was a German patrol consisting only of four men. "It's good to see you guys, we were worried we were not going to make it back to our lines," the leader of the patrol said.

"It's good to see you guys made it back, we can't afford to lose any more men," Sven said to the soldier. Hans had a funny feeling in his gut, something wasn't quite right. He couldn't put his finger on it but something was just out of place.

CHAPTER TWENTY-FOUR

HANS NOTICED THEIR UNIFORMS, they were German but they were Wehrmacht uniforms (regular army) not SS. The Wehrmacht front lines were miles away, what were Wehrmacht doing clear over here Hans wondered to himself. Hans leaned over to the SS soldier to his left and softly said, "Notice anything odd about these guys? They are Wehrmacht uniforms, not SS." The SS soldier looked at the patrol's uniforms and realized Hans was right. The SS soldier asked the leader of the patrol in Russian, "How did the patrol go comrade?"

In an Eastern Russian accent the leader of the patrol said, "It went well comrade, we . . ." then realized he had just given himself and his men away. The Russian soldier quickly raised the barrel of his rifle in an effort to get the first shot off at the SS men. The Russian fired and the round grazed the right arm of the SS soldier the Russian had been speaking to. Suddenly all hell broke loose and the Russian and SS soldiers began to fire at each other at point blank range. None of the men on either side had time to reload their rifles before the fight became a deadly hand to hand free for all.

The Russian soldiers were outnumbered six to four and they were surprisingly quickly subdued with three killed and one captured. Two SS men each grabbed one leg of the surviving Russian soldier and began to drag him by his feet back to the

Wiking headquarters for interrogation. They were followed by another SS man who occasionally would give the Russian a swift kick to his head as it was dragged across the rocky ground. They graciously wanted to make sure that his welcome to the German lines was as memorable as possible.

Early the next morning a Russian aircraft was flying overhead dropping propaganda leaflets on the German lines. Several of the leaflets floated down to the ground near Hans and Sven's foxhole and Sven quickly reached out of the foxhole to retrieve one. Sven sat back down in the hole and began to read the propaganda the Soviets had sent them telling Hans what was written on them. "It says here that the Russians are proclaiming the inevitable and ultimate victory against the Third Reich. It also says that General von Seydlitz-Kurzbach who was captured at Stalingrad and many other high ranking German officers in a group called the Alliance of German Officers are pleading that those of us trapped here in the pocket surrender. That we will be fed, treated well, and welcomed as brave new Soviet comrades. Gee, Hans, it sounds wonderful. What do you think should we do, should we go over and surrender so we could experience the warm hospitality of our new Russian brothers?"

"No, Sven. It sounds awful nice. Russians are warm and gracious people as we both know but I am not very fond of Russian food. Carina's cooking is much better so I think I am going to have to turn down the offer," Hans said to Sven.

"You always have been a picky eater, Hans. There is a big delicious world out there. You should be more open in trying new things. You know they say variety is the spice of life," Sven said raising his brows at Hans.

"That's okay, buddy, I'm not much on spices either," Hans replied.

"Hans, you are such a prude," Sven said playfully rolling his eyes.

A Russian artillery barrage began raining down on the Wiking defensive line near the village called Shenderovka. The barrage meant only one thing, there was going to be a Soviet assault on the village. Wiking only had three Panzer tanks for the defense of the village and they soon had to pull out due to the concentrated fire of artillery.

Once the pounding of the Russian artillery stopped, the infantry assault began. There were thousands of Russian soldiers screaming like mad men running toward the SS line of defense. The Russian assault was supported by seventeen T-34 tanks and they were headed toward Hans and Sven's position like a bat out of hell, stopping only to take aim and fire at both the village and the Wiking defensive positions.

The SS inside the village were loading the wounded on anything that would roll. The few trucks and support vehicles they had were overloaded with injured soldiers and they desperately began to use carts to evacuate as many of the wounded as possible.

The Wiking men on the front line fired at the Russian hoard that was determined to overrun the SS positions. It was as if no matter how many Russian soldiers they killed more and more kept coming, multiplying like rabbits.

Ammunition became very low and it was clear that the Russians would inevitably take the village and it was time for the Wiking men to make a hasty retreat. Hans slapped Sven on the back of his helmet to get his attention amongst all of the chaos that was going on. "It's time, buddy, we got to get the hell out of here!" Hans yelled in an effort to be heard over the defining sound of gunfire.

"You don't have to tell me twice, try to keep up with me, sweetheart," Sven said as he slapped Hans on the cheek and then quickly jumped out of the foxhole and sprinted off.

"That idiot," Hans said to himself. Hans could hear the bullets quickly whizzing by overhead. "Son of a bitch," Hans said with both anger and fear. Hans reluctantly crawled out of the foxhole and when he thought he might have half of a chance to get away he leapt to his feet and ran like hell as fast as his legs could carry him. Sven was waiting for Hans around the corner of a building just inside the village. Hans ran to where Sven was waiting for him and sat down panting heavily from his quick retreat.

"What the hell took you so long, did you see an old friend or something?" Sven asked angrily.

"Shut up!" Hans said still trying to catch his breath. The boys got out of the village as fast as they could and tried to meet up with the rest of the SS and attempt to break out of the pocket to safety. They met up with other scattered German soldiers, some SS and others Wehrmacht. They formed two lines of fourteen thousand men each and began to march through a corridor that they thought they might be able to squeeze through to safety. Once the columns made it through to what they thought was safety, many of the men began to cheer and fire their weapons into the air in celebration. As they did a battalion of Russian T-34 tanks began to close in on the columns from both sides. At first the T-34s fired at the columns killing many German soldiers, but soon the tanks were too close to one another to fire without hitting another T-34.

The Russians began to use their tanks to run over the German troops. The troops scattered in a frenzy of fear as the tanks ran over the wounded soldiers in the carts. The men began running in all directions in order to save themselves from the horror of being crushed by Russian tank treads. There were men screaming for their mothers as they lay on the ground, the lower halves of their bodies crushed from the treads of the tanks. Arms and other body parts of the German soldiers stuck to the tracks of the T-34s, going round and round as the tank moved from soldier to soldier killing them in droves. By the end of the carnage twenty thousand German soldiers lay dead, their bodies mangled beyond recognition. Hans and Sven were among the few that survived, they hid until they thought it was safe to continue on to the safety of the still German held territory.

The Soviet victory in the Korsun–Shevchenkovsky Offensive marked the successful implementation of the new Soviet battle doctrine. The breaking through of Germany's forward defenses allowed fresh Russian reserves to drive deep into the German front. The arrival of large numbers of American trucks, tanks, and half-tracks gave the Soviets much greater mobility than they had earlier in the war. This, coupled with the Soviet capacity to hold large formations in reserve gave the Russian Army the ability to drive deep behind German lines again and again.

Though the German front did not totally collapse like Soviet command had hoped it did cause a significant deterioration in the strength of the German Army on the front. The loss in German tanks and artillery, nearly all of which was lost during the breakout was unrecoverable for Germany. Throughout the rest of the war the Russian Army would place large German forces in jeopardy time and time again. The Germans were stretched thin and they had to constantly make attempts at extracting themselves from one crisis to the next. The new mobility gained from American troop transport trucks decisively aided in the Soviet offensives they conducted and were now the trademark of the Russian Army for the remainder of the war.

Hans, Sven, and many other retreating Germans reached the Gniloy Tikich stream. The stream was fifty feet wide and about six feet deep due to melting snow. The panicking men desperate to escape saw the river as their only option. The last of the tanks, trucks, and wagons were driven into the water and the soldiers felled nearby trees to make a makeshift bridge allowing fleeing troops to flounder across. Hundreds of men drown, being swept downstream with horses and other military debris. Many soldiers that attempted to brave the water went into shock from hypothermia due to their bodies being exposed to the freezing water.

Hans and Sven amazingly survived all of the deadly challenges thrown at them and made it back to the German lines at Lysyanka. About a mile from the town there was a platoon of Einsatzgruppen SS who had captured ten Jewish men. The Einsatzgruppen soldiers formed two lines in front of the Jewish men and at the end of the two rows stood one SS soldier holding a Luger pistol on the edge of a large bomb crater created from a recent bombing by the Russian air force.

The Jewish men were forced one by one to walk between the two lines of SS men toward the crater. The Jewish men were beaten by the Germans as they walked through the two lines of SS being hit with the butts of their rifles or poked and cut with their bayonets. The cuts were not enough to kill them but just enough to bring them great pain. Once they had reached the crater a smiling Einsatzgruppen soldier would put his pistol at the back of their head and pull the trigger, their lifeless bodies falling one by one into the deep crater.

This seemed to give the SS man with the pistol great joy, laughing as he ended the life of each one of the Jewish prisoners. "They are some sick bastards," Sven said to Hans in disgust. Hans and Sven watched for a moment, wishing there was something that they could do to save those poor souls that were having their lives so brutally stolen from them. They both knew that if they attempted to interfere, they, too, would end up at the bottom of that crater.

"Come on, Sven, there is nothing we can do here," Hans said ashamed of being associated with the murderous Einsatzgruppen SS. The boys hungry, cold, and tattered, remorsefully turned away from the grizzly seen and continued their march to Lysyanka.

Hans and Sven made it into the village of Lysyanka and discovered there were hundreds of other tattered and starving soldiers that had escaped the Cherkasy pocket. They had eaten everything in the village, including the food of the local inhabitants.

Every hut and building was full of German soldier seeking refuge from the cold and there was nowhere for the boys to rest. Hans spotted a small house. Most of the house had been blown away from an exploding artillery shell but a small corner of the kitchen was still standing. Hans and Sven decided that being the only type of shelter, it would have to do. "Sven, help me clear some of this rubble away and we can sit next to the wall and get out of this damn cold wind," Hans said with his teeth chattering from the bitter cold.

"Good idea," Sven replied eager to get any relief possible from the biting winter wind.

CHAPTER TWENTY-FIVE

THE BOYS BEGAN CLEARING away the rubble and Sven discovered next to the wall on the floor covered with dirt and debris, a half loaf of bread. The bread was very moldy but at this point they were so hungry they were willing to eat anything they could find. "Hans! Look, some bread!" Sven said loudly.

"Keep your voice down or we won't have it for long," Hans said trying to keep the discovery from the other starving soldiers. Hans and Sven sat down and leaned against the wall.

Sven tore the moldy bread in half. "Here you go, buddy, don't eat too fast you might get a tummy ache," Sven said handing half of the bread to Hans and as usual making a joke about the situation. The boys smiled at each other and began picking the mold off the bread making sure they didn't tear off any of the bread that they could possibly eat. What remained of the bread that was edible Hans and Sven ate as discretely as possible to keep from being seen by the other starving soldiers that would kill in order to have something to eat.

"I never thought I would say this but that dirty moldy bread was delicious," Hans said as he patted his stomach.

"It's nice to see that your pallet has finally developed a taste for finer cuisine," Sven said smiling at Hans. Hans and Sven heard a tank start its engine just on the other side of the wall they were sheltering against.

"Hey, come on," Hans said as he stood up. Let's go see where that tank is headed." The boys ran around the wall to the idling tank on the other side.

The tank commander was standing on top of the tank about to crawl into the turret. "Hey!" Hans yelled at the tank commander. "Where are you headed?"

"We were ordered to go to Lublin to regroup and be reinforced with more men and tanks," the tank commander said.

"Can we catch a lift with you?" Hans yelled up to the commander.

"Sure, climb aboard," the tank commander said waving his hand to the boys to climb on top of the tank.

Hans and Sven struggled to crawl up the side of the tank then huddled next to the turret. "Hang on, ladies, we are going to go as fast as this old girl can take us," the commander said. Then he gave the driver the order to move out. As the Tiger lumbered down the road Hans shouted at Sven attempting to he heard over the roaring engine, "This is the way to travel!" Hans said as he was bouncing around from the tank driving down the rut filled road.

"Nothing but first class for us, my friend," Sven said as he tried to keep from being thrown off the tank from the violent rocking and swaying. Hans and Sven hunkered down behind the turret in an attempt to hide themselves from the chilling wind but their efforts were to no avail, there was no escaping the bitter cold. It was going to be a long cold and uncomfortable ride but that was a small price to pay for salvation.

The boys arrived in Lublin feeling as if they were frozen but grateful to be alive and out of Lysyanka. Hans and Sven made it to the German staging area and immediately went in search for food. Hans spotted a sergeant smoking a cigarette supervising a supply truck being unloaded by four privates. He was overweight, his uniform was clean and pressed and he looked as if he hadn't spent a day on the front the whole war. "Hey, Sergeant, where can we get us something to eat?" Hans asked exhausted, famished, and desperate for any kind of sustenance.

"Boy, you two look like hell," the sergeant said very femininely for a soldier. Hans and Sven looked at each other a little confused at the sergeant's distinct sounding reply. "We just broke out of the pocket. We barely got out of there alive," Hans replied. "We haven't had much to eat in a few days. Could you please tell us where we could get something? We are really hungry."

"Sure, I'm sorry boys. There is a mess tent just around the corner," the sergeant said. I'm sergeant Oden, you can call me Odi. You boys get your bellies full and come back here to see me. I will get you some new uniforms and show you where you can clean up." Hans stuck out his dirty hand to shake the sergeant's and said, "Thanks, Odi, we sure appreciate it." The sergeant looked at Hans's filthy hand and reluctantly shook it. As Hans and Sven made a sprint around the corner the sergeant pulled a white lace lined handkerchief and wiped the hand that he used to shake Hans's with. Odi then stuck out his arm as far away from himself as he could and with pinky in the air, proceeded to shake the handkerchief free of dirt, looking as if he were a southern bell from a plantation in Georgia attempting to get the attention of a potential gentleman suiter. The boys made it around to the mess tent and rushed inside. There was no food being served and the only person in the tent was a private gathering the dirty pans from the previous meal in order to wash them in preparation for the next.

"Is there anything left to eat, Private?" Sven asked the young man.

"No, I am afraid not. We do have a few field rations left in the back of the tent in a crate you're welcome to."

"Thanks!" Hans and Sven said at the same time, and then the boys bolted like startled horses out of the tent as fast as they could to find the field rations. They found the crate, took the lid off to get the food they so desperately needed, but there was only one box of rations left. They would have to split the meal designed for one man between them. It wasn't the first time they had to share a meager amount of food with one another and from the looks of the way the war was going it wasn't likely the last. The rations were called *eiserne* portions or (iron portions). These were issues of rations for times where daily resupply could not be guaranteed such as raids or other missions. The rations consisted of small packs of hard biscuits, a tin of *leberwurst* (enriched meat spread) and ten grams of *milchkaffee* (instant coffee; this was a combination of coffee and milk and it was seen as a proper energy drink for the hard fighting SS troops).

Hans and Sven sat down and leaned against the crate to share their meal. "Sven, do you remember when we were kids and we would each scrape up some change and we would combine what money we had together and buy a chocolate bar to share?" Hans asked.

"Oh, yeah, I remember that. I also remember the trouble we got into for sneaking off and doing that," Sven said and they both laughed remembering back those days so many years ago."

"This kind of reminds me of that," Hans said. "We have shared just about everything with each other over the years. You're an idiot, Sven, but I love you, buddy," Hans said.

"That's great," Sven said, "But you're not going to try and kiss me, are you? Because I'm a married man now."

"No," Hans said. "I'm not going to kiss you until you've had a shave and a bath. You're filthy and smell like a pig." Hans and Sven smiled at each other with a brotherly affection for one another, and then got back to dining.

After Hans and Sven finished up eating their meager rations, they headed back over to the building where they met Odi. The boys walked through the front door of the building and just inside was a very large room with uniforms, canteens, shovels and just about any other item a soldier would need in the front. Odi was sitting behind a desk on the left side of the room with the typical picture of Adolf Hitler on the wall behind him.

"Heil Hitler!" Odi said with the Nazi salute. "Did you boys get you something to eat?" Odi asked.

Hans and Sven reluctantly raised their arms and returned the salute. "Heil Hitler!" the boys said with little enthusiasm. "All they had was one box of rations and we had to split it. Can't complain though, it's better than nothing," Hans said to Odi.

"That's the spirit," Odi said. "We all have to make sacrifices for the fatherland right now, but I hear Hitler has his top scientist working on a new wonder weapon that will turn the war around and we will rid ourselves of those dirty Bolsheviks once and for all."

Ever since the war had turned into the ally's favor, the troops were told that Hitler had new wonder weapons in development and that they would be deployed right around the corner turning the tide of the war into the Reich's favor. Surprisingly, many of the troops believed this propaganda even when defeat was inevitable until the end of the war. Hans and Sven had become disillusioned from what they had seen and experienced in the war and had a hard time believing anything the great Third Reich told them now but they were still hopeful in the defeat of the Russians.

"Odi, could we get some uniforms and some new boots and then direct us to where we can get cleaned up?" Hans asked. "I didn't notice this outside but besides looking dirty you guys are, let's say a bit aromatic," Odi said making a stink face. "I will get you what you need then you two dirty boys get out of here, you're stinking up the place. I don't want some young handsome…I mean, some officer coming in thinking it's me smelling so pungent."

"Sorry, Odi," Hans said. "Are there some showers or somewhere we can take a bath?"

"About a block down the street on the left you will see a red brick building. Right behind the building they have set up showers for the men. The showers are outside and it's cold but they heat the water up for you so it's actually not too bad," Odi told them and then he went about his business grabbing the uniforms and boots for the boys. Odi gave Hans and Sven their new boots and uniforms. "Here you go, boys. Now you two little stinkers go wash up," Odi said smiling at Hans and Sven.

"Will do," Hans said. "Thanks for all your help, Odi."

"You are welcome, boys, you two be careful out there," Odi said. Odi and the boys gave each other a small wave goodbye then Hans and Sven headed out the door to the showers.

"Wow, what did you think about that guy?" Sven asked.

"Well," Hans said. "I think he would be perfect for looking after your girl back home. I don't think there is a chance in hell of him trying to steal her from you." Hans and Sven looked at each other and chuckled then headed directly to the showers.

Those relatively few like Hans and Sven in the Wiking division that managed to escape the Russian encirclement were very lucky to survive but in doing so Wiking had lost all of its armor and a great deal of equipment and men. The remaining men and equipment that managed to survive the Russian onslaught in the Cherkassy Pocket were formed into a Kampfgruppe unit. A Kampfgruppe was an ad hoc combined arms formation that consisted of a combination of tanks, infantry, and artillery including anti-tank weapons.

CHAPTER TWENTY-SIX

AFTER ARRIVING IN LUBLIN Hans and Sven were given a chance to recuperate from the hell they had gone through at the front due to the reformation of the division. The days quickly passed and a winter of horror and desperation were exchanged by the men for a spring of rejuvenation and hope. On a beautiful day early March of 1944, Sven was relaxing on his cot daydreaming about home when Hans excitedly entered the room. "Sven!" Hans said. "I got a letter from Carina."

Sven quickly sat up. "Did I get anything from Elsa?" Sven asked with anxious hope on his face.

"No, buddy, I'm sorry, you didn't. Hey, but I will read you what Carina wrote maybe there is news about Elsa in it as well," Hans said trying to console Sven and raise his spirits a little. Hans began to read the letter.

My dearest Hans,

First I want to say that I love you very much and miss you terribly. I hope you and Sven are both okay. Elsa is here with me and we are both writing this letter together so make sure Sven is with you when you read it.

"Hey, buddy," Hans said. "You got a letter after all, it's for me and you."

"That's great," Sven said. "Shut up and read."

"Okay, relax," Hans replied.

Hans, I don't know how to tell you this but I will just come straight out and say it. You are now the proud father of a beautiful baby girl.

"Woohoo!" Hans yelled. "Can you believe it? I'm a father!" Hans said beaming with pride.

"Well, what's her name daddy?" Sven asked almost as excited as Hans.

"Uh, right, let's see. She says . . ." Hans looks at the letter trying to find his place where he had last read.

"Here it is," Hans said as he found the spot on the paper where he had left off. "Her name is Olivia and she is beautiful. Corina says thank god she looks like me and not you." Hans laughs.

"She is right, you know. She would be one ugly girl if she looked like you," Sven said as he gave Hans a light punch on his arm.

"Carina said that's not all the news they have for us. Elsa wants Sven to know he is a daddy too. He now is the father of a handsome baby boy named Liam."

Sven sat there as if he had seen a ghost. "Well, dummy, aren't you going to say something?" Hans asked surprised from Sven's silence.

"I don't know what to say," Sven said as if in a daze. "I never really thought about me having a kid."

"Well, your happy, aren't you?" Hans asked.

"Of course I am read on, read on what else does it say?" Sven asked biting at the bit.

"It says here that Liam looks like a mixture of both you and Elsa but he definitely has your thick dark hair. She also says that like you he is very vocal on his needs and partial to my breasts." The boys look at each other with smiles from ear to ear and then continue reading soaking up every delightful word. "She also said that she loves you and can't wait for you to come home and meet your son."

"Can you believe it? We are both dads!" Sven said to Hans.

"I just hope Liam doesn't turn out to be like you," Hans said. "Oh, and by the way, keep him away from my daughter."

"I can't promise you that, buddy," Sven said. "If she looks anything like his mother I don't think there will be much we can do to hold him back. I'm expecting that he will be a chip off the old block," Sven said proudly.

"Let's hope not," Hans said. "One juvenile delinquent in Osby is enough."

"Let's go see if we can find us a drink, I think we deserve a toast for ourselves," Sven said to Hans with a grin.

"I have to agree with you, buddy," Hans said with a smile. "We do deserve it."

At the same time as the reformation of Wiking was being conducted, in the north the Soviets threw nineteen armies and two tank armies supported by thirteen hundred aircraft at the Germans. This in an attempt to push the German forces all the way back to the Vistula River in Poland. Hans, Sven, and the rest of the Wiking Division were to be hastily transferred to Poland and amalgamated into a reformed Fifth SS Panzer Division Wiking. The Wiking Division was to take part in the desperate attempts along with the Third SS Panzer Division "Totenkopf" to try and stem the Soviet advance.

Before the men of Wiking were to begin their journey to Kowel they were to gather and get in formation for a briefing and new orders. As the hundreds of SS men stood in formation in the streets of Lublin they began to talk with one another wondering what was going on. They could all tell something big was about to happen due to the urgency of the formation but did not have a clue on what it could be. "I wonder what the hell is going on," Sven said quietly as he leaned over to Hans.

"I'm not sure but it looks like we are about to find out, here comes the sergeant," Hans replied.

The highest ranking sergeant of each company of SS men stood in front of their company they were assigned to. "*Achtung!* (Attention)" The sergeant bellowed. All of the men standing in the formation snapped to attention at once and the distinctive sound of the men's boot heels coming together echoed down the length of the street. Each man raised his arm in a Nazi salute to the captain "Heil Hitler!" the men shouted in unison.

The captain of the company walked over and stood in front of the formation facing the men. Returning the salute the captain said, "Heil Hitler!" Then the captain shouted, "*Ruhrt euch!* (Stand at ease)". Without any delay the captain began addressing the men in a stern and authoritative tone. "Near Poland our army is in great danger of being overrun. The Russians have begun a new offensive and our men are greatly outnumbered. Our job will be to quickly assemble and go west to reinforce our units there and conduct a large and decisive counter offensive. Wiking has been tasked to hold Kowel, a key railroad junction one hundred and sixty miles from Warsaw in the Pripet Marshes. We must stop the enemy's advance and keep the Russians from reaching Warsaw at any cost. I am not going to lie to you and tell you this will be an easy task, it won't. We must do our duty for Hitler and the Fatherland bravely giving each of our lives in battle if necessary. Heil Hitler!" the captain again shouted followed by a Nazi salute. The SS men in formation snapped to attention at once. "Heil Hitler!" The men shouted returning the captain's salute. "*Entlassen* (dismissed)!" the sergeant shouted at the men, and the men were released from formation.

"Well, buddy, what's your take on that?" Hans asked Sven.

"I think we are going to be in deep shit when we get to Kowel, is what I think," Sven said as if he was absolutely sure of his reasoning. "What's your opinion, Hans?" Sven asked curious of Hans's view of the upcoming situation they inevitably were going to be in.

"I think you are absolutely right," Hans said. "This war isn't turning out like we or the Reich quite thought it would. The Russians have taken back just about every area we overran and defeated the bastards and they seem to have an endless supply of weapons and men. Germany's running out of men and equipment, fuel is scarce and it is almost impossible to get resupplied with the food and ammunition we need. The situation is looking bleak my friend," Hans said with a clear sound of worry and dread in his voice. They stood there for a second looking down at the ground thinking about the dangerous crusade they were about to embark on. "Come on, Sven," Hans said as he put his hand on Sven's shoulder. "Let's get our gear together and give our rifles a good cleaning before we head out. We need to make damn sure they are in good working order. From the sound of it we are definitely going to need them."

The boys headed back into their barracks to clean their weapons and prepare for the journey to Poland. It was the first time Hans and Sven had a fear about an upcoming operation, the both of them had a lot to live for now. They were not just two carefree boys on an adventure anymore. Their lives had drastically changed from those reckless and carefree days they lived with no responsibilities. They now were husbands and fathers, with new responsibilities and needed to stay alive to take care of them.

At 3:00 a.m. the next morning the men were awaken by their platoon sergeant yelling at the top of his lungs. "Get up, girls! It's time to move out, get your asses downstairs and get in formation. We are going to march to the station and board the train to our new home in Poland. Let's go! Move it! Move it!"

"He is such a sweet and caring man. Kind of like a loving father figure that we can look up to," Sven said with his typical sarcasm.

"Shut up, dumbass, and grab your gear we have to get downstairs," Hans said unusually gruff.

"Damn, Hans, did you wake up on the wrong side of the bed this morning?" Sven asked.

"I'm sorry, Sven. I had a hard time sleeping last night. I had this crazy dream that's kind of confusing, I didn't quite understand it but I know it was scary."

"What was it about?" Sven asked very curious.

"I was in a city that was pretty much destroyed from bombing and German soldiers kept falling from the sky and hitting the ground dead," Hans said with a very concerned and confused look on his face. "There were skeletons sitting up out of their graves laughing and pointing at the falling soldiers and there were Russian soldiers leaning against the front of their tanks smoking cigarettes laughing at the skeletons laughing at the German soldiers falling from the sky."

"That is weird," Sven said. "I think you might have finally totally lost it, buddy." "Shut up, dumbass let's get downstairs," Hans said to Sven.

"I can tell it's going to be shits and giggles traveling with you today," Sven said sarcastically. Hans gave Sven a go-to-hell look, grabbed his gear and headed down stairs to the formation. Sven soon joined Hans and the platoon marched to the train station. Hans's platoon climbed aboard the train and sat down in the seats inside the railcar.

All of the soldiers were unusually quiet and there was a very somber atmosphere in the railcar. It was as if they all had the same feeling as Hans and Sven about the upcoming operation and the men's morale was at an all-time low. Happy or not this mission was going to take place and the men were disciplined and dedicated enough to give their all in the fight. Not for the Reich but for their buddy beside them.

The train for Warsaw pulled away from the station leaving the Korsun Cherkasy Pocket disaster far behind and transporting the men to a brand new nightmare. SS Wiking still had no heavy weapons after coming out of the Cherkassy Pocket and were only equipped with small arms and machine guns. There was no doubt in the men's minds that they were grossly outgunned and outnumbered by the Russians and that there stood little possibility of holding the Soviet juggernaut from taking Kowel, Warsaw and eventually Berlin itself but they had no choice in the matter they had to continue the fight.

CHAPTER TWENTY-SEVEN

THIRTY MINUTES OUT OF Lublin, Ukrainian partisans attempted to ambush the German transport train Hans and Sven were on. The partisans open fired on the train with small arms fire mostly rifles with a couple of machine guns in an attempt to kill as many Germans as possible on the train. A round from a rifle pierced the window next to Sven and the bullet went through Sven's garrison cap knocking it from his head and on to Hans's lap sitting next to him. Sven look at Hans with shock on his face. "Holy, shit! Sven said. "That was close, that bastard almost killed me."

Hans picked up the cap off his lap and looked it over. There was a bullet hole through the cap and Hans stuck his finger through the hole and wiggled his finger. "It looks like someone doesn't like you, Sven," Hans said jokingly. "Did you piss off some Ukrainian girl?"

"I know I broke a lot of hearts when I got married but I didn't think anyone would take it that bad," Sven said as he took his cap back from Hans and closely inspected the hole. "It's a good thing they weren't aiming a little lower it would have gone clean through that hole in your head and killed me. Look at that damage to the window you caused. How are you going to pay for that? You don't have any money and you are not getting any from me, you're on your own, pal," Hans said with a stern look on his face.

"I am going to tell your wife that you are being an asshole and she will correct that piss poor attitude you have. I guaranty it, buddy, so you just better watch out," Sven replied.

Hans reached into his breast pocket and pulled out half of a chocolate bar he had been saving. They were hard to get on the front and they were a rare treat for the men when they were lucky enough to get one. Hans broke the half bar in half again. "Complain, complain, and complain. You bitch more than a woman," Hans said. He handed Sven half of the chocolate. "Here, put this in your mouth and shut up, you're giving me a headache."

Sven took the chocolate from Hans. "Admit it, Hans, you love me and you know it," Sven said then took a bite of the chocolate and gave Hans a smile.

Hans rolled his eyes and shook his head then leaned back in his seat. "I'm going to try and get a little shut eye while I can I would suggest that you do the same, I don't think we will be getting much sleep after we reach Poland," Hans said as he closed his eyes.

"Good idea, buddy," Sven replied. Sven put the last bit of chocolate in his mouth then he, too, leaned back in his seat to get a little sleep chewing the last of his chocolate with a childlike smile on his face.

Hans and Sven reached Warsaw and were set up in a camp on the edge of the city. Just before dawn after only a few hours of sleep Hans and Sven was awaken by the bellowing of their platoon sergeant. "Get up boys! Drop you cocks and grab your socks and get your asses in formation. It's time to earn your pay. Let's go! Let's go! Move it! You look like a damn bunch of old women. Let's go!" The men in the platoon scurried around putting on their uniforms, grabbed their equipment and rifles and quickly got into formation.

"Boy, he's in a good mood this morning," Sven said sarcastically.

"I understand why," Hans replied. "By the looks of things he got less sleep than we did."

The platoon got into formation in front of the platoon sergeant who was standing in the road in front of the platoon's tents impatiently waiting with a very unpleasant scowl on his face. "Listen up, ladies," the platoon sergeant said. "We are to load up in half-tracks and conduct a patrol on the west side of the city. There are partisans ambushing patrols and we need to lure them out into the open and take care of the problem."

The sergeant then broke the platoon up into squads and pointed each squad to the half-track that they were to board for the patrol. Hans, Sven, and the rest of the squad were assigned to the last half-track in the row of vehicles. The line of half-track started their engines to get underway. The half-track Hans's squad was on didn't quite sound right when the engine started, there was a distinct knocking sound from the engine. "Boy, this thing sounds like a piece of junk," Sven said with a stink face.

Hans grinned and gave a little chuckle. "It looks like it has been through hell and back too," Hans replied.

The half-tracks began to move out and get underway on their new mission. Fifteen minutes into the trip the half-tracks engine began to sputter causing the vehicle to repeatedly lurch then come to a complete stop from engine failure. The driver tried again and again to restart the vehicle but it was no use, the engine was completely inoperative. The driver then got on the radio to inform the vehicles ahead of them the situation but the radio wasn't working as well.

The driver then turned around to the men in the back of the half-track and said, "Well, guys, it looks like we may be here a while, the engine is dead and the radio is too. Might as well get comfortably or get out and stretch your legs, who knows how long it will be until the patrol realizes that they have lost us." Some of the men relaxed in the back of the half-track but most of the men climbed out of the half-track and a few of them lit cigarettes struck up conversations with one another.

On the opposite side of the road near a treeline on the other side of a small field were hundreds of men, women, and children standing in a line guarded by Einsatzgruppen SS men. The Einsatzgruppen were making them all disrobe and in groups of twenty then they were directed to stand in front of a six foot wide, ten foot deep, and thirty foot long trench that the SS had forced the captive men to dig.

Men, women, and even small children were lined up facing the trench, babies in their mother's arms crying as their mothers tried to comfort them as best as they could. Hans and Sven could hear the mothers and other women crying and begging the SS men to spare their children's lives but their pleading was to no avail. A line of Einsatzgruppen soldiers all fired at once with their rifles at the defenseless people and their bodies fell into the trench in unison.

The babies that were still alive would suffocate to death under the weight of the next row of victims' shot. This would continue until the trench was full of bodies then the SS men would have the prisoners cover the trench with dirt and dig another. Then they continued the slaughter until their gruesome job was complete leaving no one alive. "How in the hell could someone do that? Hans asked Sven. "They must all be insane."

"I know," Sven said. "Can you imagine if it were Carina and Elsa, with our children?"

"I don't even want to think about it," Hans replied. "Those poor people, this isn't right." By this time the whole squad was watching, their attention directed to the sound of the shots fired by the Einsatzgruppen soldiers. The mood of the men became somber and they hung their heads in both sympathy and shame for being, even if indirectly, a part of this inhumanity and horror.

Later that day, Hans's stranded squad caught a ride back to camp on an Opel Blitz truck, a German Army utility truck that was headed back to Warsaw. By the time the squad got back to camp it was just before dusk. The men were told that the lieutenant, the platoon sergeant, and half of their platoon were killed by a partisan ambush, killed by those they intended to kill. The entire day filled with sorrow and dread. The remaining men of the platoon that were not killed were given leave until resupplied with men but only a local pass, they could not leave Warsaw.

The next morning Hans and Sven decided that they would venture out and see Warsaw more as a tourist than a soldier. Hans and Sven set out to see the Theatre Square, the Great Theatre, and the historical Jabłonowski's Palace. The seat of the president of Warsaw but what they found was a devastated city. Many parts of it in ruins from the invasion and frivol destruction at the hands of the German Army. "When I was a boy mom and dad brought us to Warsaw on holiday," Hans told Sven. "This looks nothing like what I remember. If you didn't tell me where I was I wouldn't have a clue it looks so different."

"More and more when I see a place like this or even how these civilians are treated, I think to myself, what if this was back at home?" Sven said. "I'm not feeling right about this war anymore, Hans. I don't like what is going on and I am not sure if I believe in what we are doing anymore."

"I know, buddy," Hans replied. "I am feeling the same way about things but I am not sure what we should do."

"Let's get out of these uniforms, get some civilian clothes and get our asses back home," Sven told Hans.

"We would be caught before we got to the coast and shot for desertion," Hans said. That's just not an option."

While walking around amazed at the devastation of the city the boys stumbled across a small boy sitting against the railing on a bridge. He was little more than skin and bone, clearly on the verge of death. Hans had a *Bahlsens Leipnitz,* a cookie leftover from the chow hall he was saving for a snack and gave the cookie to the young boy. The boy raising his arm as if it took all the effort he could muster gratefully took the cookie from Hans's hand. The boy gave Hans a smile then took a small bite of the cookie. Hans could tell the boy enjoyed the cookie very much by the joy you could see on the young child's face. The boy then leaned back on the bridges railing slowly chewing the small bite he had taken. The boy's hand dropped to the ground and the cookie came out of his hand.

"Oops!" Hans said smiling from the boy dropping the cookie. "I will get that for you." Hans bent down to retrieve the cookie and give it back to the boy. "Here you go, son," Hans said as he was handing the cookie to the boy but there was no response from him. The boy was gone. The smile Hans had faded away, he was just too late to save the boy. Hans's head hang low as he was kneeling in front of the boy's lifeless body. "Another innocent child dead because of this damn war," Hans said grieving for the boy.

"It will be okay," Sven said putting his hand on Hans's shoulder. You made his last few minutes of his life pleasant. You took his mind off his misery," Sven said in an effort to comfort his friend. "His life was sad but you made his death happy and he didn't go alone, he had you."

Hans picked the boy up unto his arms and carried him off the bridge. Hans laid the boy's little body on a cart with hay in it that was just off to the side of the bridge. He ran his fingers through the boy's hair and gave him a gentle pat on the top of his head then turned away. Hans and Sven walked quietly down the street and headed back to camp, they had seen all they wanted to see of Warsaw.

CHAPTER TWENTY-EIGHT

AFTER A BRIEF PERIOD of rest and refit in Warsaw, the Fifth SS Wiking was ordered to aid other units in Kowel in the defense of the city which was under threat of an attack by a strong Soviet force in a new offensive. General Herbert Otto Gille led the men of the Fifth Wiking SS Panzer Regiment that now was equipped with newly arrived Panther tanks along with the Third Battalion, SS Panzergrenadier Regiment Germania into the battle.

Hans and Sven arrived at the front and began to aid in the defense of Kowel. Hans, Sven, and the rest of the men of Wiking began setting up a defensive perimeter in and around the city but the Russians threw wave after wave of attacks on the German lines pushed Wiking into the city of Kowel. It became clear to the Wiking units that until relief forces could materialize, Kowel would have to be defended from within. It was to become what Hitler called a fortified city.

Hans and Sven took up positions at the farthest point of the east side of the city. Hans and Sven were keeping watch from their foxhole on Russian movements when a runner, a young soldier that runs from unit to unit relaying messages came to their position. "Do you guys have a radio over here?" the runner asked.

"Yes, we do," Hans replied. "Why?"

"Goebbels has a message for our troops here in Kowel and command wants everyone to listen to the speech to build morale," the runner told Hans.

Joseph Goebbels was a German politician and Reich Minister of Propaganda in Nazi Germany. Hans and Sven had learned that Goebbels was a blow hard and that you couldn't believe a word the man says. "Great, like things aren't bad enough we have to listen to the ramblings of that idiot," Sven said shaking his head.

"That's not all," the runner said. "Word has it that we have been surrounded by four rifle divisions."

"Fantastic," Sven said sarcastically. "We are now encircled by the Russian Army and once again caught in a pocket by a brilliant Soviet pincer maneuver. Oh, that news is much better. I was starting to get bored. What kind of idiot is running the show here?"

"Just remember to listen to the speech. It was a direct order from the general himself. It looks like the speech is going to start in about ten minutes," the runner said. "I have to get going I have several other platoons I still have to tell. Good luck, guys," the runner said.

"Good luck, kid," Hans replied. "Sven, fire up that radio and see if we can get radio Berlin."

Sven grabbed the radio and turned it on. Sven began turning the dial on the radio but all they heard was static. "I can't seem to get anything," Sven said struggling with the radio.

"Keep trying," Hans told Sven. Sven continued to turn the radio dial back and forth then suddenly got a signal from the radio station.

"Hey, hey, we got it!" Sven said excitedly.

"Wow! Sven, are you excited to hear Goebbels's spiel?" Hans asked with a smile.

"Oh yeah, I'm a big fan from way back," Sven replied.

"It sounds like the speech is about to start," Hands said. "Turn the radio up just a little, Sven."

Sven turned the radio up and the speech began. "Praise be to everything that makes us hard. Hard times call for hard hearts. Whenever the Fuhrer talks to us he demands endurance and hardness from us. Never give up the struggle, never, even if everything appears hopeless. Fling the empty cartridge into the face of the enemy. Take him with you if you have to die. Everyone must be able to march, to suffer hunger and thirst, to sleep on bare ground and endure all hardships with cheerful courage. Heil Hitler!"

"That was supposed to be a motivational speech to raise morale?" Sven asked not believing what he had just heard. "That man sounds insane."

"I am beginning to think they all are crazy back in Berlin. Who in their right mind would continue a fight they know they could not win?" Hans asked in disbelief of how the Nazis were running the war.

"Uncle Adolf would, that's who," Sven said. "We need to get our asses out of here and back home before we go up in flames with the glorious Third Reich."

"I'm beginning to think you're right, Sven," Hans said. "I am definitely beginning to think you are right."

Hans's platoon was assigned to place anti-tank mines and anti-personnel mines on the outskirts of the city in preparation of an all-out soviet tank assault on Kowel. Hans and Sven both grabbed two anti-tank mines and carefully made their way about three hundred yards away out into a field on the edge of the city to strategically place the mines so they could destroy any Russian T-34 tanks that may try to enter the city from that direction.

Hundreds of mines were laid in front of the Wiking positions giving the men a small but false sense of security. "What do you think, buddy, you think all those mines will keep those Russian bastards back?" Sven asked Hans.

"Honestly, no, I don't," Hans replied. "You know as well as I do that the Reds have more men and equipment than we do. We have no air support like they do and there is little to no chance of us being resupplied. Honestly, if you truly want my opinion, we are screwed."

"You don't have to be that honest," Sven replied. "Better not say that in front of anyone else, they will shoot you for defeatism."

"You don't have to worry about that, I am not going to do anything that will get me a premature death, I want to get back home to Carina and my baby girl. You better do the same," Hans told Sven.

"You don't have to worry about that," Sven replied. "Those crazy days are over for me. I have someone to go home to as well."

The silence of the front lines was interrupted by the sound of Panzer tanks and T-34s firing at each other followed by the sound of many aircraft approaching. It was a start of a new Russian offensive codenamed Operation Bagration after a Russian general that had fought Napoleon. The offensive was vast. The Russians threw one hundred sixty divisions consisting of one point two million men, more than four thousand tanks and self-propelled guns and supported by some six thousand Soviet aircraft.

"Oh crap!" Sven said both excited from the sight of the aircraft and fearful of what was about to come. "Look at all of those planes. It looks like you could jump from one plane to the next." Bombs began to drop from the aircraft and Hans and

Sven could hear the whistling sound of death falling through the air above them. "Get down!" Hans yelled at Sven pulling him to the bottom of their foxhole. The two men got down as low as they possibly could at the bottom of the foxhole as the bombs began to explode all around them. The sounds of the explosions were deafening and seemed to go on and on, then suddenly nothing but silence except for the ringing in their ears.

Hans and Sven both stood up in the foxhole to ready themselves for a full out Russian assault. Looking around the boys saw a landscape that looked like the lunar surface and the remnants of buildings in large piles of rubble. Looking across the field they expected to see hundreds of Russian troops but to their surprise there was nothing. In the distance they began hearing the fire from Russian artillery and that told the boys everything they needed to know.

It was almost customary for the Russians to fire an artillery barrage followed by a tank assault and a wave of screaming vengeance seeking infantry. The Russian artillery shells came raining down on Hans and Sven's position and it was just as deadly as the air bombardment from the Russian air force. Again the boys hunkered down at the bottom of the foxhole for the minimal protection it provided against the devastating explosions all around them.

"I think they are mad, Hans!" Sven screamed at Hans trying to be heard over the noise of the explosions.

Hans smiled at Sven. "Just keep your ass down until it's over," Hans replied.

The barrage lasted fifteen minutes before it subsided. The boys quickly stood up and again ready themselves for the Soviet assault. Across the field in front of them hundreds of T-34 tanks came barreling out of the tree line but they were met with German Panther tanks and an all-out slug fest broke out between them.

The tank battle lasted thirty minutes and at the end of the battle the Russians had lost one hundred and three T-34 tanks with minimal loss of German tanks. As the T-34s sit burning in the field an all-out Russian infantry assault began. Thousands of screaming Soviet soldiers was running across the open field weaving between the burned out wrecks of T-34s. Once the Russians were within range the Wiking men opened fire on the Soviets with machine gun and rifle fire mowing down the enemy by the dozens but wave after wave of Russian soldiers kept coming.

The Russians continued to advance across the field and when they reached the minefield the Germans had laid whole groups of them would be killed when one of their comrades stepped on a mine. The wholesale slaughter of Russian men did not detour them from continuing their attack with reckless abandon. They had no regard or fear of losing their lives in their effort to take Kowel. Though they were the enemy Hans did admire the bravery the Russian soldiers displayed.

A young SS runner came to Hans and Sven's foxhole. "Hey, you two," the runner said trying to get the boys' attention away from the assault.

"What is it?" Hans asked the young man.

"We are pulling out," the runner said.

"We are pulling out now? Hans asked. "This is a hell of a time to move out we are in the middle of an assault."

"Those are the orders," the runner said. "We are encircled and we have been ordered to break out and regroup in Bialystok about one hundred and ten miles northeast of Warsaw."

Hans and Sven looked at each other very confused at the orders. "Hey, it doesn't break my heart," Sven said. "Let's get the hell out of here while we can."

"Orders are orders," Hans replied. The boys climbed out of their foxhole and ran as fast as their feet could carry them away from the front lines. This tactical withdraw as it was called may had just saved their lives. There was no longer anything that could stop the coming Russian onslaught.

After the desperate breakout from Russian encirclement at Kowel, the men of Wiking were allowed a short respite at Bialystok then the unit was transferred to the Modlin fortress just outside Warsaw. The Wiking division was to join the newly formed army group Vistula, fighting alongside the Hermann Goring Panzer Division. The Wiking division annihilated the Red Army's Third Tank Corps and the advent of the Warsaw Uprising brought the Soviet offensive to a halt.

CHAPTER TWENTY-NINE

The Russian Army held back hoping the pro-western resisters and the German Army would destroy each other, then the Russian Army would enter the city to mop up the remaining enemy whether it be German or pro-western resistance. This allowed the Germans time to destroy Warsaw including its civilians and the home army. Hans's company was assigned to eliminate the resistance in Warsaw. On patrol in the city Hans, Sven, and the rest of their platoon was ambushed by resistance fighters. Gunfire began coming from both sides of the streets from hiding positions in the rubble of buildings.

The buildings had previously been destroyed by the German Army on orders from Hitler. They were to raise the city from the face of the earth and kill everyone in it. Bullets began to rain down on the platoon some hitting the ground around Hans and Sven, others killing members of the platoon. "Son of a bitch," Sven said trying to duck the incoming fire. "Let's get the hell out of here." Sven grabbed Hans by the shirt sleeve and quickly pulled him around the corner of a partially standing red brick building.

Many men of the platoon, few of them having any combat experience still stood in the middle of the street firing back at the well-hidden resistance fighters. "Get the hell out of the street!" Hans yelled to the men but they could not hear him over the gunfire. Sven shook his head and said, "Dumb asses" then ran out into the street under heavy fire and directed the young Wiking men to seek concealed fighting positions.

Sven grabbed the soldiers one by one pointing them in the direction they should go and when he had all of the men off the street he ran back to the position he and Hans were at. "What the hell do you think you were doing, you idiot?" Hans yelled at Sven with a scolding look on his face.

"Well I..." Sven said before he was interrupted mid-sentence.

"I don't want to hear it, you moron. Keep your ass down and don't do anything stupid like that again."

"Okay, okay," Sven reluctantly replied.

"Get a grenade ready and follow me," Hans said to Sven.

Hans led the way around to the back of the building and they quietly climbed up the rubble to where they could see several resistance fighters by the windows of two rooms. The back half of the rooms were blown away from an explosion so the view was clear and unobstructed from Hans and Sven's sight. "You throw your grenade in the room to the left and I will throw mine in the room to the right," Hans told Sven. "On the count of three, one...two...three...throw!" Hans and Sven threw their grenades in the two rooms. The grenade that was thrown at the room on the left went unnoticed but the grenade thrown in the left room was spotted by one of the resistant fighters. The resistant fighter picked up the grenade in an effort to throw it back at Hans and Sven but before he could both grenades exploded almost simultaneously killing everyone inside both rooms. Hans and Sven then went behind the next building. It was in the same condition as the first building but instead of two rooms occupied by resistance fighters there were three. Hans and Sven only had one grenade each on them. "Here is what we are going to do," Hans said. "You throw your grenade on the room on the far left and I will throw mine on the far right. Try to get your grenade as close to the wall that connects to the center room and I will do the same on the other side. Let's see if we can knock down three birds with two stones. Ready, one … two … three … throw!" Both grenades went exactly where the boys were trying to throw them and they landed unnoticed by the resistant fighters. Again both grenades exploded simultaneously. Flying shrapnel from the grenades went through the walls and killed everyone in all three rooms.

"I can't believe it!" Sven said excitedly. "Your crazy idea worked! You're pretty smart for a country boy."

"You're right," Hans replied. "And let's not forget who the smart one is."

The small arms fire coming from the resistance fighters ceased and they slipped away avoiding capture by the men of Wiking. Hans and Sven walked back around to the front of the buildings then they and the remainder of the platoon gathered and aided their wounded comrades. The remaining men in Hans's platoon made it back to camp, cleaned up and got themselves something to eat. After the men had eaten their meal, Han's squad was called to a meeting by their platoon's lieutenant.

"Our platoon is going to stand down for a couple of days until the men that we lost will be replaced," the lieutenant said. "The day after tomorrow this squad is to report to the Einsatzgruppen for special duty. They are understaffed and overworked and need men to take on the overflow." Hans and Sven knew exactly what the lieutenant meant by "special duty." Hans and Sven looked at each other with dread and disbelief on their faces. "Get some rest while you can. That is all, men, dismissed," the lieutenant said.

The squad broke up and went their separate ways and Hans and Sven quietly began to speak to each other. "What the hell are we going to do, Hans, you know neither of us can do that. Killing the enemy is one thing, murdering women and children is another," Sven asked sincerely concerned about the situation that they were about to be in.

"I don't know, buddy. If we refuse we will be shot, no doubt about it. I don't know what the hell we are going to do," Hans replied with despair in his voice.

"I have an idea," Sven said a bit excited. "I can get us a couple of leave passes, by the time they figure out we are gone we can be out of the country on our way home."

"Now, how in hell are we going to get two leave passes?" Hans replied with sarcasm clearly expressed on his face.

"I know a guy that works at headquarters and he can get us some passes," Sven said.

"What the hell makes you think that he will give you two passes smart guy?" Hans asked.

"I have something on him that is sure to get us some passes." Sven boasted.

"What could that possibly be?" Hans asked.

"Back at the Korsun Pocket I saw him put a bullet in the back of his lieutenant's head."

"You're shitting me?" Hans asked not quite believing what Sven was claiming.

"That's right, I saw him plain as day and he knows I saw him so, I shouldn't have any trouble getting them whatsoever."

"Boy, if you can do that you might just save our asses," Hans said.

"I think I will pay him a visit right now as a matter of fact, and then we can get our asses out of here right now," Sven said with determination.

"Good luck, buddy, I hope this works," Hans said with concern.

"I don't need any luck at all with this one don't you worry, consider yourself on your way home," Sven replied confidently then quickly walked away with almost a childlike skip in his step.

Hans paced back and forth occasionally kicking a rock out of his path while he waited for Sven's return. After about an hour Sven return walking slowly toward Hans with a look of defeat and despair on his face. "I'm sorry your idea didn't work, buddy, it was a good idea though," Hans said trying to make his old friend feel better.

"No, that's not it, Hans, I'm just trying to figure out a way to tell you ... we're going home!" Sven said as giddy as a schoolgirl waving the two passes in front of Hans's face.

"You dirty bastard," Hans said with a smile giving Sven a bear hug. "I can't believe it, we are going home," Hans said grinning from ear to ear.

"Let's get our shit and get the hell out of here," Sven said.

"You are such an eloquent man, Sven. I find it hard to believe you're not an officer."

Hans and Sven both gathered their things and quietly left camp and made their way to the railway station to catch a train to the coast. Presenting their leave passes to the guards at the station they were allowed to board a supply train to Kaliningrad East Prussia. The ride wasn't very pleasant or comfortable due to having to sit on crates of rations on a cargo car but any sacrifice would be made for their escape.

"What's the first thing you want to do when you get home, Hans?" Sven asked as he rocked back and forth from the train rolling down the rails of track.

"Well," Hans said. "After I spend a little time with Carina I am going to sleep for a week in a nice soft bed. What do you want when you get home?" Hans asked.

"You know what I want. I want a big glass of fresh milk and a plate of eggs," Sven replied.

"That does sound good," Hans replied with a smile.

The boys settled back and got as comfortable as possible. The rocking of the train and the white noise of the wheels going over the rails of the tracks soon put them both to sleep. The train arrived in Kaliningrad and the boys got off the train and began looking for transportation to Baltiysk, a coastal town in East Prussia where they might be able to catch a boat to Sweden. Hans and Sven were walking through the city when they passed a bakery. On display through the window they could see beautiful cakes, cookies, and other pastries. The both of them were very hungry and the sight of these tasty treats was almost too tempting to resist.

A gruff voice from behind them ordered them to show him their papers. The boys turned around and were face to face with two Gestapo men, Nazi secret police well known for their bloodlust and brutality. "Your papers, please," the Gestapo ordered. Hans and Sven slowly retrieved their papers and handed them to the officer. "I noticed by your cuff title you are Wiking SS, you're a long way away from your unit," the Gestapo officer said.

"Yes," Hans said. "We are on leave and going home for a couple of days."

"I don't think that is possible, all leave on the Easter Front has been canceled for weeks now. I am afraid you two are going to have to come with us," the Gestapo man ordered as he grabbed Hans by his arm.

Hans and Sven looked at each other with desperation on their faces. Without hesitation or second thought Sven quickly pulled his pistol from his holster and shot both Gestapo men in the face. The sound of the shots being fired alerted a group of German soldiers about a block down the street and they immediately began to run toward Hans and Sven to investigate.

The boys turned away from the soldiers and made a desperate attempt to elude the soldiers pursuing them.

The boys ran down the street until they came to an alleyway that would lead them to a parallel street. They kept looking back but the soldiers didn't seem to follow them, either that or they had quickly lost them. Either way Hans and Sven were quite all right with it and a bit relieved. Hans spotted a truck heading in the same direction as Baltiysk and waved the driver down to see if they could catch a ride.

The driver stopped the truck next the Hans and Sven and leaned over in his seat to roll down the passenger side window. The driver was an older man with grey hair and a thick grey mustache. "You boys okay? Are you in some kind of trouble?" the driver asked.

"No, sir, we are just trying to get a lift to Baltiysk. Are you heading anywhere near there?" Hans asked the man.

"As a matter of fact that is exactly where I am headed. I will give you a lift but you boys will have to sit in the back, my passenger seat is taken by old Kaiser Wilhelm here," the old man said lovingly scratching his old German Shepherd behind his ear.

"Thank you, sir, we are very grateful," Hans said to the man. Hans and Sven climbed into the back of the truck and they were underway.

Once they reached Baltiysk the truck driver dropped the boys off about a mile from the peer and they had to walk the rest of the way.

CHAPTER THIRTY

Once Hans and Sven got to the shoreline they spotted a fisherman working on his nets near the docks. Hans and Sven walked up to the fisherman. "Excuse me, sir, do you know if any of the boats will be sailing to Sweden anytime soon?" Hans asked.

"No, son, no one heading to Sweden, but there is an old Finn at the end of the dock and he is heading to Finland soon, you might be able to catch a ride with him to Finland. His boat is the last one at the end of the dock. You will know it's him when you see an old man with grey hair and the biggest belly in northern Europe," the man said with a grin patting his belly with both hands.

The boys smiled back at the man. "Thank you, sir," Hans said and the boys hurried down the dock toward the boat. They got to the boat and saw the captain doing last minute preparations to get underway.

"Boy that fisherman was right," Sven said to Hans. That has got to be the biggest belly I have ever seen."

Hans laughed then shouted out to the captain, "Sir!" Hans said trying to get the captain's attention.

"What do you need, boy, can't you see I'm about to get underway?" the captain said gruffly.

"The fisherman at the end of the dock said that you were sailing to Finland, could we please catch a ride with you?" Hans asked.

"I take it from your accents your Swedes," the captain said.

"Yes, sir, we are trying to get home," Hans replied.

"Climb aboard, boys, it will be nice having a little company for a change."

The boys climbed aboard and were soon underway. "What the hell are a couple of Swedish boys doing in the SS?" the captain asked.

"Well, sir, when Germany went to war with Russia we thought we would join the Waffen-SS to fight the communists, it didn't turn out to be such a good idea," Hans told the captain.

"Well, it's a good time to go home, boys, and very wise. I hear the Germans are getting their asses handed to them on three fronts. That Hitler is nuts, I could tell it from the beginning. I heard him give a speech back in 1931, I could tell then the man was crazy then but he seemed to have everybody fooled. People will believe most anything if they are told it enough," the captain said. "Let's get underway we are burning daylight. You boys can sit back here on the aft of the boat for the trip."

The boat got underway, it was a beautiful day and the baltic was calm, perfect for a day at sea. Hans and Sven sat and talked during the voyage about things they would do when they got home and how they couldn't wait to see their new children and play with them.

The boat got close to Finnish waters when a German patrol boat come speeding up behind them. "Halt and prepare to be boarded for inspection," ordered one of the sailors over the German patrol boats megaphone.

"Bullshit," the boat captain said. "Those Nazi bastards aren't coming on my boat," the captain gave the boat full throttle to get to Finnish waters before the Germans could catch them. The German patrol boat fired a burst of machinegun fire over the bow of their boat and gave them one more warning to stop the boat so they could be boarded.

The Vainamoinen, a Finnish Navy Panssarilaiva (an armored ship) for coastal defense, saw what was happening and fired a warning shot across the bow of the German patrol boat. Being outgunned the German patrol boat immediately broke off the chase. Sven jumped up excited celebrating evading capture when the German patrol boat fired one more burst from machinegun at the boat. One of the rounds fired from the machinegun entered Sven's back and exploded out of his chest.

Sven fell to the deck of the ship convulsing, bleeding profusely and gasping for air. Sven screamed, "Hans! Hans! Where are you?"

Hans was in shock at the sight of his best friend lying on the deck with a clearly obvious fatal wound. After all they had been through. Not this, not now, so close to home. Hans ran to Sven and knelt down beside him and cupped his hand under Sven's head lifting it slightly off the deck.

"Take me home, Hans," Sven said shaking, with desperation and panic in his voice.

"We are going home, buddy, just hang in there," Hans replied trying to comfort his old friend.

"Promise me, Hans, promise that you will take me home," Sven said slowly weakening.

"We're going home, buddy, just hang in there," Hans said with confusion and fear.

"Promise me, Hans, promise me you will take me home."

"I promise, buddy, I am going to take you home, Sven, I swear."

Sven stopped convulsing and gasping for air and smiled lovingly at Hans. "Teach my son how to be a good man, Hans, teach him to be like you." Sven took his last breath and it slowly left him. Sven's lifeless body went limp in Hans's arms. Sven was Hans's childhood friend and his buddy through thick and thin. A man that would gladly walk through hell with Hans and bravely stand at his side through any torment the devil could throw at them. A brother that had risked his life to save Hans's time and time again without any regard to his own life and now, suddenly, he was gone. On his knees Hans held Sven and cried with more anguish in his heart than he had ever experienced or thought possible.

Hans held Sven in his arms until the boat pulled into the port in Finland. At the dock the police were waiting for the boat, the Finnish Navy had radioed that their boat was headed into port and the authorities were there to greet them. A middle aged man with a three-day beard met Hans on the dock and showed Hans his badge. "I am officer Antero, please come with me, son," the officer said as he grabbed Hans by the arm and led Hans to an awaiting car.

When they reached the police station officer Antero led Hans to a small room with a table and two chairs, one on either side of the table. 'Sit down," the officer ordered. Hans sat down in the chair. Hans was still numb from the loss of Sven and was in a mental state of shock and didn't really care about what was happening to him. "What's your name, son?" the officer asked.

"My name is Hans, Hans Grubber."

"You know you made a big mistake deserting and coming to Finland SS, man. We have a treaty with Russia now you know. That's right. We are all buddy buddy now. All the old squabbles we had between each other are all forgotten. Now when you SS desert and come here, we turn you right over to the Russians. Where they're going to send you, I am sure you will never come back from, my friend. That is if they don't shoot you first. Empty out your pockets and put everything on the table," Officer Antero ordered. Hans stood up and reached into his right front pocket and pulled out a pocket knife and some change. Hans then took his billfold out of one of the pockets in the back of his pants and put it on the table. He then reached into the right pocket of his shirt and pulled out a small pencil and a letter that he had started writing to Carina. Hans then reached in his left shirt pocket and pulled out his lucky medals that he was awarded during the Winter War of '39. Officer Antero immediately recognized them as Finnish medals for bravery. "Where did you get those medals?" Antero asked.

"They were awarded to me in the Winter War. I was wounded at the battle of Suomussalmi."

"Suomussalmi?" Antero asked. I was in Suomussalmi in 1939. We were in the same battle."

"Small world," Hans said nearly emotionless.

"Oh, this change everything, my friend," Antero said. "I'm not turning a Finnish war hero over to those Russian bastards. Where are you from, son?"

"My friend and I are from Osby, Sweden, sir," Hans replied.

"Then Osby is where you're going, son. I will make sure of that," Antero said.

"Sir, could you please help me get my friend Sven home too?"

"I sure will, son, don't you worry I will take care of everything. I have to get you out of here as soon as I can though so no one finds out what I am doing but I promise you and your friend will be home by tomorrow evening I guarantee it," Antero said patting lightly on Hans's hand that was folded across each other on the table. "I will send someone in with coffee for you. I have a few calls to make and in a couple of hours I will take you and your friend to the train station."

"Thank you, sir, I really appreciate your help," Hans said gratefully. Antero left the room to make the calls necessary to coordinate everything that needed to be done to get Hans and

Sven home. Hans sat in the small room and as he waited he thought of Sven and all of those crazy, wonderful things they did together over the years. Hans's emotionless face began to turn into a smile thinking of his childhood companion and the trouble the two boys couldn't seem to keep themselves out of.

The hours drifted by as Hans tried to reflect on every memory he had of Sven. Antero came back into the room. "Okay, son, time to go. Come with me," Antero said to Hans. Hans followed Antero out of the building and the two of them got in a car and headed for the rail station. "I arranged a coffin for your friend and he is being taken to the station now. Your train will be leaving in an hour. You're on your way home, son," Antero said to Hans.

"Thank you, sir," Hans said.

"It's my pleasure, son," Antero said with a smile.

As Antero drove Hans to the train station they talked about the Winter War and the experiences they had both good and bad. They arrived at the station and Antero walked Hans inside to the ticket booth. Antero got the train tickets for Hans and gave them to him. "I'm sorry about your friend, Swede. Good luck, kid, I hope you have a good life," officer Antero said as he offered his hand out to shake Hans's.

"Thank you for all of your help, Antero, I will never forget you for what you have done for us," Hans replied as he gratefully shook Antero's hand. Hans stood there silent, deep in thought as he watched the men load his childhood friend's coffin aboard the train. The boys were finally going home. The dangerous journey they had been on was finally over. One of the boys would spend the rest of his days in peace and the other would for eternity.

≈ THE END ≈